I0772618

THERESA BIEHLE

TALE OF TWO CURSES

OTHER BOOKS BY THERESA BIEHLE

Legend of Ghaleon Series

Spirits Entwined (Book 1)

Stars Calling (Book 2)

Novelette

Tree in a Heather Field

TALE OF TWO CURSES

BY

THERESA BIEHLE

ACKNOWLEDGMENTS

Thank you to everyone who read this early and provided their feedback! A special thanks to my cats who kept my lap warm and let me pet them as I pondered what to write next.

PROLOGUE

On a time before time was recorded...

A starstorm raged on a moonless night over a small town on Alir. It was a vicious one. The wind howled as it whipped through rows of houses, and the latched shutters rattled as they fought to stay closed in an effort to keep the falling star debris outside. No matter how hard they tried, the old and battered shutters still let in glimpses of the light blazes that hailed the shaking thunders. As long as those shakes remained from the thunder and not from a meteor slamming into the ground, most of the town would be okay in a few hours when the storm passed.

All except Jax and his family. Jax sat at his desk in his house, head in his hands, as he thought about what to do. Instead, his mind reeled hopelessly on useless thoughts. How had such good intentions gone so wrong? He had jumped in too fast and not thought about the problem from other angles, but he *had* to have done what he did. He pounded a fist on the table. He couldn't waste time on regrets now. What he cared about most had been at stake, Lila. He knew that he had to choose to try and heal not only her but the others in need as well. Unfortunately, his medical training had not prepared him for this outcome in the slightest.

He looked down at the ring he had crafted, currently held tight in his hand. The town's blacksmith had made the setting, but Jax himself had cut the gem to reflect and absorb light exactly as he had learned from the books that he had been reading. Books from the library in the green witch's village ensconced in the densely wooded area beyond this magicless town.

The cut of the gem was supposed to let in starlight, but not let it out. The starlight would charge the piece of the petal from the fabled starflower that Jax had put into the gem. He had accomplished this by slicing a thin section out of the center of the gem and sliding the petal delicately inside before attaching the gem to the setting and trapping the flower piece within. That star-charged petal would have allowed him to make wishes come true, and then recharge it again under the starlight to make more wishes come true. If only he hadn't messed it up somehow. His masterpiece hadn't worked as he had theorized. He couldn't even get *one* wish out of it! He would have had time to fix it. He would have had time to make it right. If only one of the green witches hadn't found out about what he was doing and taken a disapproving view of his accomplishments so far.

Poor Lila. She was in the cellar with Poe, their son, sheltering from the starstorm. She wouldn't live long now without a miracle. Her disease was incurable on Krael, where Jax had come from, and he had traveled to Alir because he had heard of the mythical starflower that was supposed to grant wishes. He had taken his family through a portal to Alir to try and find this starflower because none of Jax's medical training could fix her condition.

Something was slowly eating her soul. She had gotten tangled in some dark magic as a child, but it kept getting worse with time. The others whom he had seen with her affliction ended simply as husks. Living, breathing bodies, but with no mind, thoughts, or soul to drive them. He hadn't wanted that for her, even though she had come to terms with it long ago and tried to live her life to the fullest each day. He had made this expedition to Alir to try and save her. He had even found a starflower that had exceeded his original hopes!

Jax had hesitated though. He had experienced a moment of greed at the apex of his journey. Once he knew where the flower was, he should have followed the legend's protocol. He should have brought Lila there on a star-filled night and said his wish out loud, healing her forever. But no, Jax wanted to heal *everyone*. Once he saw that there was only one flower in the vast field, he didn't want to be the one to desecrate it, for once a wish was made, the starlight within the flower was expended, and the flower usually withered and died. He had a brilliant idea as he had held a petal of the starflower between his fingers that night, admiring its unique beauty and basking in its air of hope. He knew that he had learned much from the green witch's library. He had learned so much more about the starflower than he had ever dreamed to learn from their endless volumes of books on plants, wildlife, and gemstones. Using that knowledge, he would make a rechargeable wishing ring to save everyone and still allow the magical flower to live!

He took only a small piece from one of the petals,

and the flower's glow flickered for a brief moment, but then it came back just as bright to Jax's eyes. Jax had been pleased with himself. He had been astounded by his ingenuity and brilliance. He was going to become the greatest healer that lived. A healer that was able to cure all ailments with a hint of wishing magic! He hadn't thought about the repercussions though. He hadn't thought about the others that could want to use this kind of ring, or want to destroy it, if they learned of its existence.

Jax's mind came back to the present situation. He only had a few more minutes now. He had taken the shortcut through the woods back home from the library and was able to beat his pursuer here. He had stopped briefly at his desk to catch his breath, so as not to scare his family, but he had to go to them now, or never see them again. The cellar was well hidden. He knew the witch wouldn't find it unless Jax accidentally revealed it.

He opened the door concealed beneath the floorboards in the corner of the house. He saw Lila and his teenage son huddled in the part of the cellar closest to the center of the house and furthest from the starstorm outside. He sat next to them and held them close for a moment, absorbing them into his memory as deeply as he could. Remembering their sight, their smell, their feeling…all of it. Then he pressed the ring into Poe's hand as he spoke to him.

"Keep this Poe. Keep this, do not lose it, and find out its secrets. It's the only way to save everyone. My notes are upstairs. Find them after the storm. I have somewhere I need to be, right now. If I don't come back in a day, take your mother through the portal to Krael, and bring as much of my research with you as possible." Poe, a quiet boy, nodded diligently in response.

Jax looked to Lila who was already so very weak. He brushed her hair from her face and gazed into her eyes which looked like it took far too much effort for her to open from beneath her heavy eyelids. "I love you, Lila. I am sorry that I failed you."

She smiled and looked up at him, "You have never failed me, so long as we are together, we win."

He couldn't help but smile at her. She was always optimistic, even in the worst situations.

"Please, be back soon. We need you here," she urged him.

"I'll do my best," Jax replied. Then he kissed her forehead and hugged Poe tight.

"I love you too, Poe. Don't forget that."

Jax was out of time. He stood up and left the cellar, closing it as carefully and quickly as possible. When he was sure that it was invisible, he leaped out of the shuttered window and, unable to close it from the outside, left it flapping in the wind.

Jax ran. He didn't know where he was going, but he knew that he had to get out of the town before the angered witch arrived. He didn't have long to wonder where to run before being found. Rain and stardust covered his body when he felt the tendrils of…something…grab his ankles. It tripped him, and he fell to the ground with a chest-thumping thud. The tendrils dragged him through the mud before placing him upright while they wrapped themselves around him securely. They were plant tendrils. Vines. The green witch had found him.

Thorns from the vines scraped his arms as they positioned Jax into a good viewing position for his pursuer to look him over. Both of Jax's feet were slightly raised above the ground so he could not try to use them to get away, and all of his weight was slumped onto the vines.

"I'll make this simple," a man's voice spoke from beneath a long, hooded cloak that covered everything except his muddied boots. His form suddenly lit up from a lightning strike which made him seem even more ominous standing there in the briefly lit darkness. He was holding onto a knotted wooden staff that rose taller than the man. The knots at the top of the staff had strings tied to them with tree nuts that would rap against the wooden staff as it moved. He looked like a simple wood mage from the outside, but Jax knew that the magic beneath would outshine the simple external appearance of the man.

"Give me the ring, and I'll let you and your family go."

"No!" Jax defiantly responded. He knew his son was smart. Poe would finish what Jax could not. His dream was not dead as long as that ring was safe. "Why do you want the ring so badly, anyway?"

"My reasons are not important to you. Right now, if you value your or your family's lives, then you will give me what I want."

Jax did not know which green witch this was. He had met many while studying in their library, but he knew that he couldn't give him the ring, no matter which witch he was. Jax's family was safe, so the witch's threats were idle to anyone but himself. Jax kept his mouth shut as the rain and metallic flakes continued to pour down on him.

"Fine. We will start doing this the hard way," the man threatened.

The witch used magic to grow the thorns on the vines that entangled Jax until they pierced his skin, causing his now dripping blood to mix with the falling rain and pool beneath his elevated body before seeping into the soil. The star shavings in the air burned as they touched his open cuts.

"I don't have it!" Jax screamed. Partially in pain and partially in defiance.

"That's a start," the man said in a voice that was angry, but almost bored. "Now tell me where it is."

When Jax didn't respond, the thorns grew longer and new ones appeared along the vines crossing his chest and neckline.

The man let out an exaggerated sigh and said, "I grow weary of this interchange. This is very simple. Tell me now, or you die and your family will be cursed for eternity."

"You have no idea where my family is or who they are!" Jax pulled all his bravery from his soul to defy this horrible man.

"Oh, really? Well, it doesn't matter. I will find them through your blood. You share that with them. I sense that you are truly resolved not to tell me. That is a shame. We all could have walked away from this without a problem had you just gone along with what I wanted. Goodbye, Jax. My patience has run out. I will find the ring without you."

CHAPTER 1: THE CURSED RING

Present time…

A stardust shower rained down on Alir. Shimmers of color sparkled as the light reflected off the star shavings slowly floating down towards the planet's surface in puffs of clouds that shifted aimlessly with the wandering winds. It was a beautiful phenomenon that occurred, but could also be a harbinger of great danger. It signaled a shooting star, an asteroid passing extremely close to the planet's surface, grazing the outer shell of its atmosphere. Sometimes larger, more dangerous, chunks of the star passing over would tumble away becoming meteors and crash into the surface of Alir. This meant that inhabitants had to be prepared to move quickly or take shelter during one of these spectacular events.

Flakes fell softly onto a young man's hooded, black cloak as he sat on the ground with his back against a tall tree crowned with spindly silver leaves that wriggled and danced in the wind amongst the colorful confetti of stardust. His well-worn sword was laying in the grass, close to his side, but far from his thoughts.

He scribbled frantically on a piece of parchment, determined not to let the wet ink be smudged by the falling stardust. Nimble hands clutched the small wooden slab behind the parchment, giving his quill a hard surface to push against, as close to his body as possible while still allowing his hands room to write. His hooded head arched over his work to give the parchment some sort of top cover from the precipitation.

"Brook Pellon

20 years, 11 months, 29 days left

Today marks the end of the first month since we arrived on Alir. The silver-leafed trees with flaky, white bark are a stunning decoration growing tall and slender out of the thick, emerald green grasses. The ruby, vase-like flowers have yellow trim dripping down their long, oval-shaped petals stretching into stripes. They catch flecks of gleaming stardust within pools of water collecting inside their waxy petals as they dot the forest floor in vivid bursts of color. But we must beware of the beauty that surrounds us. The metal content in the silver lining of the trees is poisonous in large quantities (though delightfully delicious in smaller tastes of tea), and drinking from the pools of the vase flowers without straining the collected stardust from the top could result in a shredded esophagus and painful food consumption until it has time to heal. In short, my descriptions written here over the past few days describe the overall feeling of the greater planet of Alir: beautiful with sinister secrets. Not unlike this cursed ring. Not unlike me.

Father's notes led me here, but I am afraid it may be yet

another dead end. A month of searching has yielded another good adventure, but no progress toward deciphering what this ring is supposed to tell me. What it was supposed to tell my father, and my father's father, and those before them. My time ticks away each day. One month has been spent on Alir. 0.2% of my predicted sane lifetime wasted here, if I leave with nothing. Possibly more is forfeit though, if I don't cut my losses and move on to another thread soon. But what if Father's notes were right, and I am just not astute enough to find the next clue? Are there other promising places for me to search on this vast planet? Are there nuances in his notes that I am missing? If he was right, how can I give up after only one measly month of searching this place? I know that my father spent his entire sane lifetime coming to these conclusions. He was driven by his passion to live beyond forty years of a good, whole life. Giving up and leaving Alir now would seemingly border on the betrayal of his life's work. I can't do that. No, I cannot give up on Alir, just yet. If I did, I could not look upon my crazed father's body at home, wandering aimlessly about the house and spouting nonsense from his mouth, without constant guilt and wondering. There must be more here for me to find."

Brook growled loudly as his chocolate brown eyes looked up from his writing and into the swirling starstorm. He gripped his wooden board tightly in frustration. He shook his brown, nearly shoulder-length curls enough to vent, but not enough to throw his hood off. He had done it again. He had let internal depression and desperation come out into his writing which just amplified it in real life. He hated it when that happened. Brook had gotten into the habit of writing a journal entry each day to record his thoughts and findings and engrave them as deeply into his memories as possible. In doing this, he hoped that maybe a part of him would remember *something* after his doomsday came, or if not him, then someone else could remember it for him. Not his child of course. He was determined to have this curse end with him and not pass it along, as his line of fathers had for generations. There would be no Pellon's line after Brook. In that fact, he was immovable. Sure, daughters had been immune to this curse, but he didn't want to chance having a son to pass along this torture to. There was always a son.

Brook removed the paper from the board and split the leaves of the sheet in half. He had concocted a way to write once and get two copies, as long as he pressed hard enough against his wooden tablet while writing. One copy was for the journal that he carried in his pack, and one copy was to leave out in the world somewhere to increase the chance that even when he forgot his own life, someone else could remember it for him. A part of him knew that his obsession with not being forgotten was silly, but he couldn't shake it. Being doomed to lose his sanity and memories at the age of forty and watching it happen to his beloved father -a man that Brook had followed on his own set of adventures in an attempt to break the curse- just like clockwork on that fortieth year, down to the very exact day, had struck a nerve inside of him. After affixing one parchment piece to his journal, he tightly rolled the other one into a small glass vial and tucked it into a divot on the side of the tree that he was sheltering under.

Brook turned his attention to the ring on his right hand that he often fidgeted with, turning it from side to side with his neighboring fingers and sometimes completely upside down, facing the gem side into his hand. It supposedly held the answer to his curse. If he could decipher it, he would not lose himself on his fortieth birthday, and he could possibly get his father to return from his madness as well. At least, that is what he hoped. It was a handsome ring. The band was a chunky build made of tarnished, antique gold. It held an exquisitely cut, rounded rectangle emerald that glinted in the sunlight.

Scripted black text encircled the gemstone which his father had traced to an Alirian language dialect before he went insane. They had not quite translated the text yet, since it was ancient beyond history books, but they thought it had to do with "the stars." On both sides of the ring, pairs of wings behind a sunburst were engraved, as though the little piece of light could take flight off of the ring at any moment. The story that was passed down through his bloodline was that this ring was given to his originally cursed ancestor, and it alluded to the knowledge that the ring itself held the key to removing the curse on his family. If only he could understand the secrets that hid within the ring, then he could have a chance to live a normal life.

His ancestors had been slowly amassing theories on how to break the curse. They were stockpiled in Brook's family's basement and sorted into many piles and drawers. A stranger could easily have mistaken his basement for a library with all the content that had been collected over the years. Just like his father, Brook had been scouring those notes and creating new notes of his own to try and solve the mystery of the ring that he stared at for far too long each day. The most promising theory that he had been following, the one his father had created, was that the breaking of the curse was somehow tied to a terrible deed that was committed by his originally cursed ancestor. No one knew what had happened to cause the curse to manifest all those years ago, but Brook's father had been fairly sure that it originated here on Alir, based on the text found on the ring. Brook had been trying to trace any breadcrumbs of his ancient ancestors here for the past month but had been largely unsuccessful.

The libraries in the big cities that he had visited did not have books recording crimes of peasant families, and Brook had concluded that if his ancestor was indeed cursed for a crime, it may not have been a crime that was punishable by law. They must have angered some sort of powerful magical being to have inherited a curse so potent and long-lived. This supposition had led Brook into the woods to search for the fabled "green witches" that the townsfolk in all the cities whispered about in awe, fear, or a mixture of both.

They were spoken of almost as mythical creatures, and descriptions of their looks varied greatly. Some believed pieces of them were reminiscent of features of woodland creatures, sporting furry ears or twisting tails. Others described them as being indetectable from a magicless human who could easily blend in while mingling and meandering within one of the crowds on a city street. Tales of their demeanors greatly differed as well. Some of the children in the streets had boasted merrily of seeing witches that would leave tidbits of food or medicine for the orphaned kids, while older folks with gray hair and grumpy outlooks would swear that they had seen one stop by in the shadows of the night to work dark magics on something that went amiss in their homes. Whatever fortune or faux pas happened, it seemed that someone would claim a green witch's hand was in the mix.

He heard some rustling in the nearby bushes and was half-expecting a green witch to reveal herself since he had been deep in thought about them. Instead, a tall, abnormally large, and muscular young man with short blonde hair and bright blue eyes that betrayed hints of red when viewed at the right angle emerged carrying some small critters and a bushel of berries for lunch. Trevi looked much different from Brook, but they were as close as brothers. Friends since childhood and both shunned by the others surrounding them for different reasons, they both had learned how to have each other's back and became inseparable at a young age. Brook's father had taken in Trevi as best as he could as a child, and so they were seasoned at adventuring together. Both of them were looking for something. Something entirely different from the other one, but that didn't mean that the answers couldn't be in the same place, so they told themselves.

Trevi had his own set of issues which made the two of them understanding and non-judgmental travel partners who were amenable to each other's nuances. Trevi was part demon. His father was a demon whom Trevi had never met, and his mother had died when he was young during an episode that neither Brook nor Trevi ever spoke about. Trevi was the nicest, most caring person you'd ever meet…until he wasn't. Trevi abhorred his demonic descent. Because of it, there were times that Trevi would get pushed too far and that small part of him that he suppressed so deeply would override his normal self. That is when Brook agreed to step in.

He had beaten poor Trevi into submission more times than he cared to admit while holding him back from committing some sort of atrocity that he would regret later, but fewer times than someone who had demonic blood really should have needed it. Trevi had asked Brook to do this for him as his friend. He did not want to hurt anyone else, and his overly massive body didn't take as much damage as normal humans did while Brook did his best to contain him during his demonic episodes. Trevi was ultimately searching for something to exorcize his inner demon so he could live a normal life too.

"Oh, I thought that growl was another candidate for lunch," Trevi teased as he arranged the morsels that he gathered by the fire pit. "Looks like it was just you."

Brook picked up a dead, downed branch that was near him and threw it in a spear-like fashion at Trevi. It hit his mark and bounced off his backside as Trevi was bending over. "Ha ha, very funny," Brook replied but was not as irritated as his tone implied. He was glad Trevi was back. Being near someone kept him from falling further into a depressive mood, and Trevi at least had a sense of humor.

"Have you decided if we should return to Krael, yet?" Trevi inquired, attempting to make idle conversation with Brook after seeing that he was in a sour mood. Brook knew that Trevi didn't care if they stayed or left, but he did like to make small talk with the usually quiet and pensive Brook. Krael was the planet that they were originally from. Neither Brook nor Trevi had shown talent in the Spirit magic that was often associated with Krael. Whether their lack of Spirit potential had to do with the other curses that they were currently burdened with carrying, or if they just weren't naturally talented, Brook wasn't sure. He honestly wasn't nearly as worried about not being able to work Spirit magic as he was being doomed to insanity in two more decades, so he rarely dwelled upon it.

Luckily, for Brook and Trevi, one of Brook's ancestors had been an honorary member of the Saliek on Krael. The Saliek had piqued the interest of the Pellons since they had a ritual for eternal life that appeared to at least one of his ancestors as a possible cure to the forty-year curse. It turned out that their ritual, even though successful in obtaining eternal physical life for that particular ancestor, did nothing to prevent the insanity that enveloped his mind at forty years old. As his ancestor had decreed before losing his mind, after 100 years of physical life, someone had kindly ended his perpetual insanity and allowed him to pass peacefully into the afterlife.

Brook's ancestor's work with the Saliek had earned them two of their black traveling cloaks that were passed down the Pellon's line. 'One for a Pellon, and one for a companion,' as the letter delivered with the gift bestowed upon them had been written, 'Since adventures are best experienced together.' The cloaks allowed for safe interplanetary travel within the same solar system. Alir was just outside of an asteroid belt that separated it from the inner planets of Thaer, Krael, and Blaet which circled a dual sun system of Ontan and Tuan. The proximity to the asteroid belt was the cause of the frequent starstorms on Alir.

Brook sighed and dramatically plopped his writing paraphernalia down onto the stardusted ground creating a puff of colors before answering. "Yes, I think we stay a bit longer and search for these green witches that are all the buzz in the towns. We should at least find out if they exist before we leave, or find out what causes the rumors of the green witches to exist in the towns. There has to be *something* magical in the wilds here that causes a few of the happenings attributed to them. Green witch or otherwise."

Trevi nodded as he was preparing the food, "Wise decision, as always, my friend."

Brook sighed again. Trevi would agree with him no matter what. He was a loyal friend. Brook's only friend. A loyal friend with nowhere else to go.

Brook pushed his selfish worries aside for a moment, "Did you happen to find anything on your search?" Trevi would know Brook was inquiring about his search for a way to exorcise his inner demon.

Trevi laughed in a jovial manner that only he could pull off with a topic so serious. He never seemed to let his demons pull on him...well, at least not until they completely pulled him under. "Naw. I looked a bit for some of those starflowers that the kids were going on about. The ones that bloom only under a night sky full of stars and are rumored to grant a wish, but nothing that matched their description graced my presence as I wandered. They are also harder to find during the day though, I would reckon, being 'starflowers' and all. The kids had mentioned that they shined in the starlight, but not what they looked like during daylight. I wouldn't be surprised if they look like some non-descript weed emitting a horrendous smell of dung in the daylight or something like that. Good camouflage, ya know."

"If they exist," Brook countered, rolling his eyes.

Trevi shot him an exasperated look that he often did when Brook was being negative for no reason.

"I'm sorry. Bad day, Trev," Brook apologized to his friend as he stood up and stretched while looking off into the woods. "A wishing flower would do us both some good, wouldn't it? Let's stay up later tonight before bedding down and take a better look for shining flowers that hopefully do not smell like dung after dark."

"All right! That's the spirit!" Trevi replied and merrily tossed Brook a roasted rump of some forest creature to nibble on with a crooked smile on his face. "Did you see any trace of those green witches that you were looking for today?"

Brook shook his head, "No, but I sort of gave up a little early today and sat down to write and watch the starstorm."

"Good for you!" Trevi encouraged him. "Take in all the wondrous events that you can, buddy. You can't spend your whole life searching. I've been thinking that you need a bit of a vacation anyway. Live now. One day, there won't be a tomorrow."

A shot of irritation prickled up Brooks' stomach. He knew Trevi was being serious and not scolding him, but having someone encourage him to do something that Brook felt guilty doing always rubbed him the wrong way. He *had* to spend as much time as he could unraveling the secrets of the ring, or else he would have no time later to live…right?

Brook gave up thinking down that path, as it would

only bother him more, and he hungrily tore a bite out of his lunch. Trevi was a good cook in the wilderness. He had to admit that. The meat was plain, but cooked through maintaining just the right amount of juiciness. The berries that he had smashed on top as a glaze complimented it well. Brook took a silent moment to enjoy the lunch and just take it in with all his senses. Smell the woody smoke. Taste the sweet berries. Hear the sizzling juices. Watch the dancing flames. Feel the firm and tender meat in his hands. When Brook did this, he felt the tension inside of him melt away as he recentered himself. Peace.

Alir had not shown them all of its beautiful, sinister secrets yet. That Brook knew to be true. He would keep searching. Above all, he had faith in his father. This was his father's work that he was carrying out. His father had been so certain that there were answers, or at least more clues, on Alir. Brook would search Alir until he found…something.

CHAPTER 2: SURVIVING A STARSTORM

$\mathcal{T}$he light of the full moon shone down onto an isolated hut in the Silvertree forest. Its magic turned the hut's walls to liquid moonlight and blessed the water vats that had been set outside and along the windowsills in loving care with its power. The vibrant moon waves played with the moon chimes on the hut's plant-filled porch creating an enchanting song of tinkles and tangs that the leaves could not help but sway along with in tune. Strange and beautiful flowers bloomed in colorful bursts to the rhythms of the moon music as the moonbeams touched their previously sealed baby buds. Puffs of pollen and sweet, seductive scents floated up into the air and were caught with purposefully strung mesh netting and upturned jars that hovered above the perfectly planted moon garden.

Inside the hut, a lone girl, barely out of her teens, hummed softly to herself as she stood with her arms spread open and face tilted up towards the heavens. Her eyes were softly closed and a content smile formed upon her lips in pure pleasure. An ease and peace emanated from the girl, as it would a person being held just right by a trusted lover's protective embrace. The moonbeams danced around her in a sparkling spectacle and played with her thick, light brown hair that fell to her hips in a mess of waves, glinting off of it in winks of sunny golds and strawberry reds that only the right light could bring out of the browns.

The moonbeams played with the girl's willing and open body and soul, reading her essence and intentions before being absorbed into her entirely. As the night went on, and she absorbed more moonlight, her skin became more translucent and began to look more and more like the liquid moonlight walls of the hut. At times, she would breathe deeply in the beams of moonlight and her smile would broaden, or she would twirl around with a bout of giggles as she let her layered brown skirt spin and flair while her gleeful, light hazel eyes beamed almost as bright as the moonlight itself. Innocence, purity, joy, and magic floated around the enchanted hut in an unbridled and wild fashion.

Back in a secluded room of the hut, behind a locked door, sat an oval wooden table covered with a silver cloth behind a navy blue curtain. On this table, sat a tidily stacked deck of ornately decorated cards circled by various colors of unlit wax candles. When the waves of moonlight hit the cards, they flew up into the air, flipping every which way in the moonbeams before three of the cards placed themselves face up on the table into a straight line, a fourth single card placed above them, and the others stacked themselves neatly to form a discard pile outside of the circle of candles.

The first card in the row was an armored man facing off against a black dragon, the most powerful and vicious of their kinds, with a large sword in his hand that looked minuscule in comparison to the size of the dragon that it was pointed towards. The card's background had a trail that swirled through mountains, forests, and swamps, with imprints of creatures sporting various snarls and sneers upon their faces. It was a card depicting a journey, adventure, and dangers.

The second card had a young woman at a fork in the road. Each road's ending was in a foggy haze that she could not see beyond. She was about to go one way, but her head was turned, attention caught by a traveling merchant's wagon with baby dragons of various colors crawling all over it that was coming down the other road that she had almost not chosen. A card signifying difficult choices, and a possible alteration of one's fate.

The third card had a menagerie of creatures on it paired off into couples. Some were staring dreamily into each other's eyes, others shared in tasks, others were actively doing something playful together, and yet others were saving the life of one of the pair that was in peril. This card was one of love, friendships, and commitment.

The fourth and final card, placed above the other three, had dragon hatchlings on it. One was just peeking an eye through a crack in its shell. One was bursting forth from its shell holding a magical wand, and another was completely free of its shell and standing with its head uplifted towards the sky announcing to the world its new existence. This card placed over the top of the others signified that the story below it would take place in a setting of new beginnings for all involved.

As the last tail of moonlight left the room, it left the green and the gold candles lit with a silver-blue flame of moonlight upon the table. A small slip of paper blew up from the table that was penned in artistic calligraphy, "Should I follow them?" It caught flame on one side from the green candle's moonflame before flitting over to the golden candle's moonflame which ignited the opposite side. The swirling currents left from the moonbeams circled the piece of paper above the card reading until the two flames met, and it burned to nothing, leaving its ashes strewn across the perfectly laid cards.

***

The starstorm continued into the night, and the stardust fell more densely. Brook had kept his promise to Trevi that they would go out after dark to look for the starflowers in hopes to find one that would grant them a wish or two. If they had planned better, last night would have been the better night to go searching because the skies had been clear, and the full moon had peered down on Alir in all its beauty and light, illuminating the way through the darkness of night. Tonight, the moon was not at its fullest, and there were dark wisps of clouds that would blot its light out right when you needed it the most. Like right now, when Brook was sure he had just heard something step lightly across the path behind them, as indicated by the sound of the quick and light crunching of dead leaves on the forest floor.

The darkness had enveloped the night as soon as he turned back to look accusatorily into the trees. He held his lantern up high to throw its light as far as it would go, but he saw nothing except the dance of shadows in the trees and heard nothing but the un-oiled creaking of metal on metal as the handle of his lantern swayed from the weight of the lamp beneath it.

"Hey, Trevi!" Brook called forward. "Do you see anything behind us?" Trevi knelt on the ground inspecting a delicate flower that *may* have been considered shining...a little bit...if you were thinking about it right...with his oversized, clumsy hands. He was trying so hard to touch it softly and carefully without damaging it as he whispered wishes to its wispy petals.

Trevi responded to Brook after finishing a long, hopeful pause following the submittal of his wish to the flower, "It was probably just a harmless night creature passing through, minding its own midnight business. If it had wanted to attack us, it wouldn't have just crossed our path. It would have caught us by surprise when given the chance." Trevi stood up from the flower, holding his lantern high to look back in the direction that Brook was facing for good measure to support his friend. "It's not like it's the full moon tonight. Everyone knows *that* is when the truly dangerous creatures come out."

Brook nodded his thanks to Trevi for taking a look. "You often mention these dangerous full moon creatures, Trevi, but have you ever encountered one? I'm starting to wonder if they are akin to the tales the people told us in the cities."

Trevi gave Brook a sidelong glance before turning back to his patch of flowers. "I have my...instincts. Anyway, if they are real, I don't want to go out of my way venturing places during the full moon to go searching for them. It's not like we miss anything from sheltering one night every so often. It's probably good for us to get well rested occasionally."

Brook wasn't going to argue with Trevi. Trevi had always had his superstitions, particularly about monsters, that Brook had worked to get along with as they traveled together. It wasn't too much of a burden. Trevi even had Brook somewhat convinced that a few of his superstitions may carry some weight since Trevi did indeed have a demon's blood within him. Maybe he could sense evil on those nights with more clarity. Brook himself did have uneasy feelings on the nights of the full moon, but he also wondered if he was just sensing his usually easy-going friend's anxiety. They had been together so long that words were no longer generally needed to convey one another's feelings.

Brook could suddenly see the forest around him in complete clarity as the night sky lit up in red and orange streaks of flickering flames. "What is that?!" Brook yelled over the roar in the sky and pointed to the fiery object that seemed to be getting bigger and bigger.

Trevi immediately turned his head to the sky and yelled back at Brook as his eyes widened and brightened in the flame's light, "RUN! That's a meteor coming this way!" Trevi picked himself up and followed his own advice as he took off into the woods, forgetting his flowers.

"Blasted starstorm," Brook thought to himself as he charged forwards on the trail that they had previously been slowly traversing. He followed the path of mowed-down vegetation that Trevi's large body had left for him to follow fairly easily. Chunks of falling stardust melted into his eyes causing them to sting and water before Brook stretched a thin, translucent piece of cloth over them for protection. It made seeing in the dark more difficult, but so did the tears in his eyes caused by the clumping stardust. At least, this way there wasn't the stinging pain from it accumulating even more.

Brook dared to look back, and what he saw encouraged him to run faster than he had ever run before. A large blazing ball of fire was growing steadily in size as it seemed to be chasing him across the forest from the sky. The flames flickered in mostly reds, yellows, and oranges, but at the tips of the flames, he could see purples, blues, and greens. That must have been from the various metals burning from the chunk of ore that the meteor was made out of. He could have stared into those colorful flames endlessly, watching them dance in their rainbow forms, but he knew he couldn't let himself become mesmerized or that beauty would destroy him and not even know he was there. Once again, Alir: beautiful with sinister secrets.

Brook turned his attention back to the path of crushed vegetation and small downed trees that he knew were Trevi's leavings. Thump. Thump. Thump. His footsteps echoed through the forest and his heart beat wildly in his chest. Brook wasn't sure which thumping was more prominent. His gasps for breath were coming harder now as he ran, and the acrid smell of smoke burning in his nostrils made him choke and stumble. He could see flashes of Trevi every so often in the distance through the trees, so he knew he had to keep going even though it was becoming harder and harder to think as he neared exhaustion. He felt a blast of scalding heat from behind him, searing the back of his neck and making his skin burn like the summer suns too hot with no shade in sight. When he looked up over his shoulder, he saw that flame had caught to the tops of the silver trees. He couldn't even hear himself think anymore over the deafening roars of falling rock and fearsome flame.

It couldn't end this way! Brook's mind protested the situation as much as it could, whatever little good that would do. He had always just assumed that he would go crazy at forty and that his life would end then. It couldn't end now. It was 20 years too soon. He didn't feel ready. He felt cheated. And most of all, he didn't *want* to die. Just like he didn't want to go crazy and forget all of who he was and what he had experienced. Just as Brook began to curse the fairness of the life he was dealt with, he heard as much as felt the meteor slam into the ground. His feet, unbidden by Brook's efforts, lifted off of the ground at the jarring impact, and a wave of compression crushed the little thoughts left in his mind with excruciating pain until it was just too much for Brook to handle anymore. Everything went black.

CHAPTER 3: MOON ANGEL

$\mathcal{S}$oft tinkling rang randomly as a slow breeze wound its way through various plants housed in homemade pottery, bountiful bottles of labeled liquids, and a large set of wooden wind chimes hanging from an overhead beam, similar to a chandelier, in the center of the garden. Each chime was painted in vibrant color with stars, moons, and various planets making it an eye-catching centerpiece nestled in the depths of the untamed jungle of a garden. Brook heard the chimes and smelled a sweet, floral aroma that eased him comfortably back into consciousness. He opened his eyes slowly and took in his new surroundings. Gorgeous chaos.

So, this was the afterlife? He was slightly underwhelmed, but couldn't argue with the overwhelming feeling of peace, serenity, and comfort that it invoked inside of him. He had found himself in an outdoor garden covered by a large wooden trellis with wisteria-like flowers hanging in curtains all around him. Beneath the trellis, there were rows of overgrown plants in various shapes, sizes, and colors. The plants twisted in and out from one another, making it hard to distinguish where one ended and another began. Some were low and placed along paths on the floor, while others were mounted up higher on benches and pedestals. Various vines crawled along the trellis, woven in with the wisteria, and splashes of color would appear where clusters of small flowers bloomed.

Next to him was a pond constructed of white stones in a rough oval shape. Water splashed down a pile of decoratively stacked rocks in a small waterfall, churning up bursts of bubbles in the pond below. Orange, white, and black koi fish swam around and clustered beneath Brook's gaze while looking up at him with gaping mouths that opened and closed when they noticed that he was admiring them. They were eagerly awaiting the food that usually accompanied a person's stare.

Brook caught a glimpse of himself in the water between the fish's greedy mouths and noticed that there were bandages wrapped around his arms and neck. How was it that he was still hurt if he was dead? That wasn't supposed to happen, was it? Not that he was an expert at dying or anything. He had never really put that much thought into what would happen after death since he was so focused on going insane before death's door opened for him. He reached down towards his image in the water as a fish jumped up, shattering his reflection into rippling pieces, and gummed his finger with its slimy mouth. His hand wretched back in response to the gross feeling, and he tore his assaulted finger and gaze away from the water a little too quickly, creating a sharp pang from under the bandage on his neck. He certainly shouldn't have been feeling pain when he was dead, right?

"Oh, he's awake now! Let's go check on him." A feminine voice rang as softly as the chimes through the garden following the loud groan Brook had given from his sudden painful maneuver. Brook looked up to see what must have been an angel, which reaffirmed the fact that he was indeed dead. Girls that pretty didn't exist in the real world, only in dreams and in death. Her hair was made of spun gold and rosy reds that accented the light brown tapestry of thick threads cascading in waves down to her waist. Her eyes were big and bright; a golden hazel that beamed the color of starlight. The smooth and graceful way that she walked made it look as though she floated effortlessly across the ground to come to greet him.

When she made it to his location, she immediately picked up his arm to investigate the state of the bandages that had started to stain a light red from Brook's blood seeping through. Brook felt his cheeks darken into a red blush at her delicate touch, but he couldn't take his eyes off of her to hide it.

Brook tried to find his voice, "Um. Hi. Um. Beautiful!" His cheeks blazed with even more heat now than when the meteor's fire had scorched him. He sounded so dumb, and he knew it. Where were his words? Why had they abandoned him now?

The angel giggled melodically, a sound that complimented the windchimes even more than her talking voice. "This is just my medicine garden with herbs, vegetables, and medical plants, wait until you see the moon garden on the front porch. Now *that* is where the real beauty exists, especially during the nights of the full moon!"

"No, no, no." Brook shook his head carefully and

took a deep breath before willing words out more coherently. "You. You're an angel. I'm only recently passed, you see. I haven't seen anything quite as enchanting as you before. Where are your wings? Are they invisible? I always thought angels had wings, but I didn't think my injuries would pass along with me to the afterlife, too. I guess I have a lot to learn about being dead. Will the pain go away soon? Is it just, like, an echo or something, or is this a way of atoning for my wrongdoings in life? Anyway, enough of my silly questions, and let me ask one that matters. What is your name, beautiful one?"

The angel paused for a moment and gently laid down Brook's arm. He thought he might have seen the hint of a pink blush creeping up onto her fair-toned and freckled cheeks. She said nothing but looked wide-eyed at him before shooting a sidelong glance towards someone else striding down one of the garden paths with bloodied bandages wrapped around various extremities. Trevi. Oh. Well, it would make sense that he was dead too. Why is he laughing so hard?

Trevi stifled his belly laugh and coughed to clear his throat before speaking to the angel as he walked up next to them, "Excuse my friend, Miss. The concussion must have affected him more than we thought. Believe me when I say that he has *never* said anything like that in his life to any other human being before now. Possibly a cat, but that isn't quite relevant now. Maybe he's a changed man or has suffered some sort of brain damage. Please, don't take any offense. We are ever in your debt for your swift and skilled help."

The angel shook off whatever trance was holding her and responded humbly to Trevi, "I was only in the right place at the right time. I could never leave a wounded soul abandoned to die in the woods knowing that I have this set up in my home." She waved around herself indicating the healing garden that they were currently immersed within.

Trevi shot Brook a warning glance, the slight glint of red peeking through the striking blue of his eyes, as he stood tall behind the angel's back just as Brook was about to open his mouth again. He closed it abruptly. Maybe he wasn't dead. Ugh. If he wasn't dead, then he had just made an incredible fool of himself.

The angel returned to her ministrations of Brook's wounds, changing bandages and rubbing salves onto patches of his burned flesh. "This will have to do for now," she said. "Nightfall will come soon, and I should be able to coax these wounds to be a bit more healed when I can channel my energies better. I'll let them heal naturally from that point forward. I am reluctant to heal them completely with magic since some bodies don't take so well to the purities of the moon. Lucky for both of you that I was carrying a large amount of healing herbs with me on my night walk. Gardens are just wonderful for home access to plants, but there is just something a little more special about the greenery that grows in the wild which compels me to harvest them every now and then. The magic within the wild plants is just that much stronger from having to survive unnurtured."

"So, it was you in the forest that night!" Brook burst out, having an 'Aha!' moment. "I knew that I heard something on the forest paths behind us. How is it that you aren't hurt at all from the meteor crash?"

The angel answered as if this was the most obvious

fact in the world, "The moon's energy protected me. It's very close to being full, and the closer that it is to a full moon, the stronger my energies are tied to that of the moon."

Brook nodded at the answer, but not quite in understanding. He looked around at the plants surrounding him, and he thought about her answer, turning the tidbit over in his mind, and examining it before responding, "Are you a green witch, then?"

Her eyes twinkled like starlight on a pool of water, and her lips turned up into a secret-hiding smile at his question. "The commoners do call us that from time to time. Some of my kind take offense to the term, but I sort of find it…endearing. I mean, I do surround myself with a lot of greenery." She swept her arms around in a grandiose manner, twirling her skirts as she spun around to gesture to the entire garden that they were in, "And, if they say 'witch' without a hint of snark in it, then it's not so bad of a word. My name is Emmeline Rosengard, by the way, not the 'green witch'. You can call me Emmy if you'd like."

"Very nice to have met you, Emmy." Brook could barely contain his excitement from bursting out. He had found a green witch! He was getting somewhere on his journey, finally. If she could protect herself from a crashing meteor, maybe she, or others like her, could be strong enough to remove the curse that burdened his family…or to have been the one to cast it on his ancestor in the first place. Brook would have to be careful and watch his steps around her. Trevi had saved him after having put his foot in his mouth earlier, but he didn't want to make a habit out of offending a powerful being capable of magic that he didn't understand. Brook figured he couldn't be blamed for what happened earlier. After all, he had thought that he was dead, and well, angels and death were tightly interwoven, right?

She had gone back to humming and tending to a few plants in the garden as Brook lost himself in his thoughts. Spirits, she *was* angelic in all ways. So much grace and innocence wrapped around the great magic within her. He didn't think he could push those thoughts from his mind. He'd just have to not voice them. She was Emmy, not an angel.

"Mooning over moon girl with your moon eyes there, lover boy?" Trevi said to Brook while elbowing a place on Brook's side without any bandages. "Never thought to see the 'sworn to be loveless' Brook smitten with a lady."

"Hey! I thought I was dead!" Brook folded his arms defiantly placing the back of his shoulders towards Trevi which just made Trevi chuckle. Brook harumphed indignantly.

"Aw, come off it now, I'm just teasing you," Trevi said, "She seems like a nice enough girl, saving us and all." Trevi lowered his voice and looked quickly over to Emmy to make sure she was fully occupied before continuing, "There is a part of me that doesn't trust her though."

"Is it the same part that is scared to go outside during the full moon?" Brook replied with maybe a little too much bite in his tone since his feelings were still stinging from Trevi's jibe moments ago.

Trevi gave him a sidelong glance with narrowed eyes and a small frown, "Yes. It just so happens to be that very part. That doesn't mean that we shouldn't be careful."

Brook's voice came out excited again, ignoring Trevi's comment about being careful, "She's a green witch, Trevi! A green witch! She has all this magic power, so maybe she can help with the curse!"

Trevi nodded, "And maybe she can give us some information on these starflowers we heard about too. She seems to know a lot about plants."

Brook felt himself beaming as he turned himself to face Trevi once again. All hard feelings were forgotten, as always seemed to happen between the two. "We have a lead, Trevi! For the first time in months, maybe years, it seems like we are making progress!"

Emmy's soft voice floated over to them, "What are you two giddy goats yapping about back there? You know it's not polite to leave your host out of conversations. If I were less of a girl, I'd send my sentrifly over there to make sure you weren't plotting against me."

"Sentrifly. Hey, Trevi, do you know what a sentrifly is?"

Emmy sighed, "And yet, he continues." With a snap of her fingers, a dazzling glow of light appeared in shades of silvery blues and flew over to Trevi and Brook. It just sat there, glowing brightly. "Well go on now, honey bees, keep on buzzing. A girl's gotta be careful with two strange men in her house. Sammy won't hurt you. She just lets me hear your conversations. No worries." Emmy turned back to her plant tending.

Brook reached out towards Sammy, and she flew just outside of his grasp, maintaining proximity. Quick little bug she was. Brook looked at Trevi who just shrugged as he said, "She has got a point. Some men aren't as good as us. She has a right to keep herself safe."

Brook couldn't argue with that, but it felt awkward talking to Trevi now that they had a known eavesdropper glowing and possibly glowering at them. He couldn't see the bug's shape or face within the light of the glowing sphere. Trevi leaned back against a stone wall of a garden behind him and let his eyes droop. He was still tired, and his body ached. He absent-mindedly twirled the ring on his finger and took it off for a moment to examine it out of habit. He glanced up at Emmy and noticed that she no longer had the shining gold and rose strands in her hair. Strange. He put the ring back on and they returned. He repeated this trick a couple of times to make sure he wasn't seeing things.

Trevi looked at him funny. "What's wrong, Brook?"

"What color is Emmy's hair to you?" Brook asked.

"Uh...brown?" Trevi replied slightly confused.

Brook handed his trusted friend the cursed ring, something he would not have done to anyone else.

"Put it on. What do you see?" Brook urged Trevi.

Trevi had to put it on his smallest finger because he was so much larger in build than Brook, but he complied. He looked around the local area as if searching for something out of the ordinary. "The same stuff as I did before. What am I looking for?"

"Look at her hair! What color is it?"

"Uh...brown?"

Brook deflated. Was he truly crazy? Trevi handed the ring back.

"Sorry, buddy. Maybe you need some sleep. It's been a rough day."

Brook wouldn't give up so easily though. He had a lead.

He raised his voice slightly to indicate to Emmy that he was getting her attention, "Emmy, can I ask you something?"

She nodded and came over to them after brushing the dirt off her hands from gardening.

Brook took a deep breath and let it out quickly before his confidence could leave him, "What color is your hair?"

Trevi smacked his palm to his forehead. Emmy cocked one eyebrow up and made a half smile.

"What?" Brook asked. "I'm serious! Your hair changes color for me when I put my ring on and off."

Emmy held her hand out, presumptuously for the ring. "May I see it, please?" She asked curiously.

Brook hesitated. Trevi and his family had been the only people that Brook had let touch the ring. Emmy wriggled her fingers back and forth on her outstretched palm, a bigger smile spreading across her face. "I promise I won't run off with it or anything, I just want to take a closer look at it."

Brook still hesitated. She offered him slightly more information, almost as a peace offering, "My hair is a light brown. Unless it's in the moonlight, then blonde and red strands mix with the browns."

That broke through Brook's defenses. That's what he saw when he looked at her. He saw the moonlight hair! He handed her the ring and immediately broke out into a nervous sweat as she carefully looked the ring over. She ran her delicate fingers over it and caressed it as she closed her eyes.

"Moon magic," she stated matter-of-factly when her eyes re-opened. "The ring is imbued with a strong magic originating from the dark side of the moon, and…it is bound to you." She looked up at Brook, her hazel eyes not betraying any answers or feelings, merely pointing him out. "It is very curious. I've never seen anything like this before. The words and symbols etched on here seem…somehow familiar, yet, completely foreign at the same time."

"My father said that they were an ancient dialect from Alir," Brook offered hopefully helpfully.

"It's possible," Emmy said. "I need to think about this. Dark moon magic isn't to be taken lightly. It is the opposite of the moon magic that I channel which is strongest during the bright light of the full moon. My magic revolves around life and imbuing positive energy and intentions into things. I fix problems not by ridding the world of the problem itself, but by changing the energy around the problem to be positive and good. The problems then find ways to fix themselves."

"Dark moon magic's strength comes during the new moon when the light of the moon is extinguished from the sight of magicless ones, but it can be found and absorbed by those practicing the magic of the dark moon." Emmy's voice darkened. "It is a forbidden side of the moon's magic that has mostly died out, and those who practice it often live in hiding. It works very similar to light moon magic, except that it revolves around death and imbuing negative energy and intentions into things. It creates problems by changing the energy around something to be negative and bad.

Problems find ways to come about in situations surrounded by negative energy." Emmy concluded her explanation, and everyone remained silent, taking in the new information.

"I'll be right back," Emmy said, as she handed the ring back to Brook and trotted off into the house.

"That ring sounds like some bad juice," Trevi said, turning to Brook.

"Not like we didn't already know that," Brook replied. "At least now we understand the 'bad juice' more."

"I always knew the moon was bad news," Trevi mused.

"Naw, you were always afraid of the *full* moon. If Emmy has it right, it's the moonless nights that should worry you more."

Trevi grunted and remained silent while rolling his eyes. Brook must have struck something in him. He would leave him be for now. Best to do that instead of provoking him more.

Brook hadn't been this excited in years. It felt like doors of knowledge that were previously closed to him were now cracking open ever so slightly, just enough for him to peek through. He was scared too if he was honest with himself. He was frightened of what he would find behind the ajar doors once his ignorance was dispelled. He had to contain that fear if he were to ever become fully enlightened and break this curse that held onto him. He hoped Emmy had the answers, or that she could at least lead him to the answers.

CHAPTER 4: DIVINATION DECK

Emmy returned with a deck of navy blue cards with white swirls on their backs. Brook couldn't see what was on the other side of them.

"These will hopefully help us to find the way." Emmy sat on the garden's ground with her knees bent to the side and waved for Brook and Trevi to join her. She snapped her fingers and Sammy's light dispersed before shuffling the cards in her hand.

"What are those?" Brook asked.

"This is my divination deck. It lets me see what the future could be. Meaning, what the future will most likely be based on current circumstances. Everyone can alter their futures, so nothing the cards tell us is ultimately truth, but they can help guide and inform us."

"Then why do you consult them, if you aren't guaranteed to know that what they say will come to pass?" Brook continued to inquire, confused by why she would do something so uncertain.

"For the knowledge that we gain through the experience. Sometimes just knowing a future can alter it. People can resolve themselves to take another path when they see something they don't like. Sometimes we walk with our mind's eye turned off, and seeing the possible consequences of that can jar us into doing more or making different choices. I could have done this divination alone, without you, but I choose to do it with you. If the cards turn up results that you don't particularly care for, then you can resolve yourself to change your path, if needed."

"I, uh, guess that makes sense. So, the future isn't set in stone?" Brook asked.

"No, but that is good news, is it not? Just think if someone showed you an awful future, completely set in stone, and you couldn't change it. How would you feel? Not so great, huh? Now, if you know you have the power to change your future, no matter what your past was, or present is, that makes seeing the future a bit more compelling. The future is a blank slate, yet to be written, agnostic of the past or present. The past can be used to find behavioral trends and social statuses which make certain outcomes more likely, but the past can never fully dictate the future, even though it may influence it."

Brook still sported a consternated look on his face.

Emmy sighed at Brook's reaction before continuing, "If it makes you feel better, the present and past are not set in stone either. Past, present, and future are just terms defining the relationship of events as they pass along in time." Emmy said in an attempt to console him.

"What? Not even the past is solidified? Now you're bordering non-sensical. I can see how someone can alter choices not made yet, but the past has already been done and lived and chosen. You can't change what happened then."

"Ah…spoken like someone who has not lived in a world of magic his whole life. Changing the past is not as easy as changing the future, that much is true, but it *is* possible. It has many more…unintended consequences…and it is not generally a turned to form of magic, but yet it exists."

"Does altering the past use dark moon magic?" Trevi asked tentatively, interrupting Emmy and Brook's conversation.

"It is what it is, and more upon it I cannot say other than it exists." Emmy intentionally avoided answering Trevi's question. "Let's play with the cards now, shall we? I do love playing with my cards! Sometimes I talk to them when I have been alone for a while just to have something to converse with. They know so very much! Everything they have to say is so very interesting."

And with that, Emmy closed her eyes, hands cupping her shuffled divination deck, and Brook could have sworn that swirls of silvery blue escaped from her palms and absorbed into the deck. She carefully placed three cards horizontally in front of Brook.

"I have asked them, 'Will the secrets of the ring be revealed?' The card on your left indicates how the answer relates to your past, the middle your present, and the right is the current future."

Brook eyed the card on his right with a burning need to flip it over immediately, and he felt his hand starting to hover towards it.

"Stop." Emmy grabbed his wrist. "The cards must be turned up in the proper order. Left first. The past always precedes the present and the future. Then the middle card for the present. Then, finally, the right card for the future." She let go of his wrist, and Brook leaned back, pausing to eye Emmy as he slowly reached for the left card this time, in case she was going to grab him again. He flipped the first card.

A man was climbing a mountain with rubble falling behind him. He was far up from the ground, and he glanced below him with a saddened expression on his face. At the top of the mountain, a red dragon sat and watched the struggling man with no intent of helping.

Emmy looked at the card and thoughtfully hummed before speaking. "This is a card of struggle and loss. Your past has been rough due to the secrets of this ring. You have lost things or people that are dear to you that may never be returned, yet still, you climb and struggle to find the answer."

Brook couldn't argue with that. That was pretty accurate. The loss of his father had never fully healed, and he wasn't sure if it ever would, but he knew he would keep on going because…well because he had to.

Brook flipped the second card over. It had a young dragon peering through some parted greenery into a reflecting pool. Behind it, unbeknownst to the young dragon, stood a larger dragon. The reflection in the pool that the smaller dragon saw was that of the larger dragon.

"A card of sudden changes and revelations. Possible traces of deceit or manipulation." Emmy explained.

"Are you saying that you're deceiving us?" Brook asked, suddenly defensive. A trait defining his usual self.

Emmy giggled disarmingly, "Well I haven't told you all of my truths, which may be what the card is implying, but you are newcomers to my life, and I do not wish to spill all my secrets to you. My interpretation of the card is that you are presently learning more about this ring. More about it than you ever have before."

Brook nodded and felt a bit anxious looking at the far right, and last, card. Trevi knocked his shoulder against Brook's, "You nervous about something?"

"These last two cards have seemed pretty accurate. Once we know the future on that last card, we can never go back from knowing. Unless someone changes our past with some forbidden magic." Brook explained.

"Yes, but Emmy says that we can alter our futures, if we don't like them," Trevi encouraged Brook.

"But you don't even like moon magic, Trevi, how can you be so trusting of it now?"

"I'm not. The way I see it is that we've got nothing to lose by flipping that card of hers. We either choose to believe what she says about it, or not, and we go along our way. Nothing evil about that. Nothing undoable."

Emmy shrugged. "I'm not misleading you concerning the meaning of the cards. That would be a curse-worthy crime in my circle of people. The moon may deny me its powers, and I would never want that. The moon is my friend. Or the elders may deem me an outcast, like the users of the forbidden dark moon magic. That would cut me off from a large backing of help and knowledge that I could fall back on now if I ever needed it. But, what both of you say is true in a way. Brook is right in that he cannot unsee the card unless a forbidden magic comes into play, but Trevi is also right in that what it says now is not the undeniable truth and that you can still change it going forward."

Brook reached towards the last card. The card with the ring's, and therefore his, future on it. He had been convinced enough by Trevi and Emmy's inputs that he should indeed go through with flipping it over. He just had to get it over with in one brave flick of his hand. He felt his chest tighten and his palms bead with sweat. Once he flipped the card over, he finally exhaled, not realizing that he had been holding his breath throughout his decision-making process.

The card had two men fighting in a heated match of swords surrounded by a circle of pikemen pointing their pointed pikes inward towards the fighting men while sending shouts of jeers and sneers all around them. Dragons blew fire from their mouths and smoke from their nostrils while perching and flying overhead to view the spectacle.

Emmy let out a small 'aw' with a sad face before explaining the card, "Your future is plagued with malicious slander, arguments, and pettiness. There is likely a failure of plans due to problems and trouble arising from these rash behaviors. I don't think you will succeed in deciphering the ring's secrets on your current path...or without help." Emmy trailed off into thought at her last statement about help.

Trevi sighed, "Maybe I should have listened to you, Brook, and not encouraged you to flip the card over. This card is clearly about me. I need to leave you if you are to succeed."

"No!" Brook all but yelled at Trevi frantically. "You can't leave me. I need you!"

Trevi was sadly standing up, clearly having

decided upon leaving for the good of his friend when Emmy called to him.

"Trevi, sit down, please. My intuition tells me that this is about Brook's behavior, not yours. He was the one flipping the cards. Trust me on this one. I have seen you two interact only briefly, but Brook needs you more than you need him. If you leave him, he will undoubtedly fail. Not only will he fail, but he will fail much sooner without you. I also believe that you will need him to succeed in what you're looking for too. Your fates are intertwined."

Emmy turned to Brook, "And you need to stop being a proper poohead to your friend. You will fail if you continue to not consider his needs as equivalent to yours."

"Hey, what was that for? I care more about Trevi than any other person!" Brook turned his frustration onto Emmy now that Trevi had sat down again.

"I've seen your actions and conversations over the last little while, and I've seen these," Emmy emptied a satchel that was previously hooked to her belt onto the ground before them. Vials filled with rolled parchment scrolls tumbled, rolled, and clattered onto the packed dirt.

"My letters!" Brook exclaimed looking about him incredulously.

"You care more about yourself than any other person." Emmy accused him in the softest, least accusatory voice possible. A voice that was merely pointing out a fact. She started reading snippets from the letters that Brook had silently penned over the last month that they had been on Alir to strengthen the truth of her words.

"Trevi is off searching for that silly starflower again. I wish he wouldn't squander so much time on a town child's musings and that he would pay more attention to finding dinner. My stomach is growling."

"Well, I mean, he…" Brook started blathering.

Emmy cut him off and read another piece of paper, *"Wasted night. Trevi is wary of the full moon, so we are forced to remain inside this dank cave until its 'evils' pass instead of traveling forward. Such a nice light it could have been to travel under."*

"Even you said the full moon is…" Brook tried to defend himself.

Emmy cut him off again, *"I tried to tell Trevi not to get his hopes up about wishes, but he still searches for the starflower ever since we heard about it. We need to focus on the ring's message."*

"He will just be more disappointed when…" Brook tried again.

Emmy continued anyway, *"Trevi is so superstitious sometimes. I feel like it brings us down."*

Brook just whined this time.

Emmy finished off with one final blow from his letters, *"Spirits crush that prideful beast! He doesn't listen to a word I say when he doesn't want to."*

Brook sat with his head bowed in defeat and arms up in the air, but finally keeping his mouth shut.

Emmy stopped reading the letters and looked up to Brook, "It's not wrong to put yourself first to some degree, and it is often necessary, but maybe try taking Trevi's starflower search a bit more seriously, and try not to prod him as much about his reservations on the moon. Those will end in a rash argument sooner or later that these cards have already concluded will end in your ultimate failure. Fill the world with positive energy instead. Help and encourage Trevi on his starflower search as he encourages you with your need to end the forty-year curse on your ring. This will make your bond stronger, and you will both be more likely to succeed with each other by your side. Succeed by helping others succeed."

A defeated Brook was finally able to get a cohesive block of words in, "You've made your point, Emmy, I'm sorry. You're right. I'll do better. Hearing you read my own words to me hurts more than I thought it would. If anyone else had said things like that about Trevi, I would have defended him in a hot-headed burst of anger. I should not say things myself that I wouldn't want others to say."

Brook pushed some loose dirt on the ground around ashamedly, "Now, that you've made your point, could you please put those vials back in their hiding places? I'd still like to leave behind a trail of my presence for someone in the future to find if I do end up failing in this ring deciphering endeavor before I turn forty."

"Even though you sound like a condescending cockatoo?" Emmy said playfully.

"Yes, even though I sound like a condescending cockatoo," Brook replied exasperated. "Maybe my new letters from this day forward will sound less negative, and whoever reads them will see a change in me."

"I like the way that sounds. Learn from the sun to rise brilliantly!" Emmy smiled her approval with the most gorgeous smile and with a poof of translucent vapor, all the vials were gone.

"Where'd they go?" A baffled Brook asked while searching around.

"Back to where I found each and every one of them. Just like you requested." Emmy responded while making a motion of plucking invisible things, presumably letter-filled viles, out of thin air around her.

"How did you find them, anyway?" Brook inquired.

"I found them while I was picking wild herbs one day, and have been following you ever since. Keeping my distance, of course. Trying to see if you were a threat. I needed to at least wait for the full moon to feel safe in approaching you, but even by then I didn't have a reason to, other than I did find your musing about the ring and your forty-year loss of mind predicament intriguing. I wanted to help in some way, but I felt compelled to ask the moon first."

"What did the moon say?" Brook asked.

"It gave me the impression, backed up with what your cards showed us today, that I would be able to aid you. I don't know what to do at the moment, but I'm sure time will tell. The moon knows, and I trust the moon. I will do what I can to help you if you'll have me along."

Brook turned to Trevi, "What do you think, big guy? Can we handle a third in our group while on Alir?"

Trevi smiled and nodded with what could have been a shine of a tear in his usually demonic-hinted eyes. He gave a slight bow of thanks in Emmy's direction.

Brook turned back to Emmy, "Of course, we will have you along with us. Thank you, Emmy. For more than just returning the vials and saving our lives."

"No worries! I don't need my divination deck to be telling me that you'll be finding more to thank me for later, but I'll bring it along anyway. I figure I at least owe Trevi a reading at some point since I've done one for you."

Trevi shook his head frantically, "No way, little Miss. I'll leave my fates unknown if that's okay with you. Too many emotional confrontations came out of Brook's reading today for me to want to do that again."

"As you wish. You will not hear about your possible fates from me unless you ask. Would you like me to tell you a bit about the starflower you seek, instead?" Emmy dangled the last bit of the sentence out there like a worm wiggling for a fish to bite.

The biggest smile ever lit up across Trevi's face, "If you have the time, I would listen to anything that you know about the starflower!"

CHAPTER 5: SEARCH FOR THE STARFLOWER

mmy and Trevi had spent the rest of the previous day in animated conversation about the starflower to which Brook had listened and absorbed as much as he could. Emmy was truly passionate about plants and had learned a lot in her short years of existence. Hearing Emmy talk about the starflower as though it existed gave Brook more faith, and he felt excitement growing within him in anticipation of their journey to locate one. Brook's excitement was only outweighed by Trevi's who just happened to be a much larger person than Brook, therefore Brook deemed it only proper that he outweighed him in something that could otherwise be considered equivalent.

Brook had recorded the details on the starflower from those conversations in his daily letters for his records so that he would not forget them. He had left most of his letter copies that he had transcribed on Alir at Emmy's place to offload his pack before starting their journey, but he made sure to take the snippet written on the starflower with him so that he could reference it, as necessary. He told himself that he would stop by her home and gather the rest of the letters before returning to his home on Krael.

"Starflower – Brook Pellon's transcriptions from Emmy Rosengard's descriptions.

- *A large flower, native to Alir, growing to be almost 2-feet in diameter when fully mature and consisting mostly of wide, floppy petals surrounding an approximately 8-inch round center base where its seeds are stored.*
- *The flower is nestled in large leaves that cup around it, hiding it during the day, and revealing the flower to the skies at night.*
- *Relatively short in height compared to its large diameter, the starflower only comes up to a person's knees, or so.*
- *Various flowers have been seen in the past adorning a wide spectrum of colors, though the petals of a single flower are generally only darker and lighter shades of one hue.*
- *Usually found in high places with little tree cover, such as mountain tops, to be closer to the stars.*
- *The pollen of a charged starflower glows at night. When the pollen is encountered without someone seeing the starflower itself, it is often called 'pixie dust' as it makes anything it covers look as though it is imbued with magic.*
- *When charged with starlight, the starflower glows with radiant light and can grant a wish to the person who delicately holds one of its large petals, as though they were holding someone's hand, and tells their wish to the flower with their words and their*

heart.

- *The wish drains the flower of its starlight charge, and therefore only one wish can be made at a time per flower.*
- *It is theorized that when the starflower charges up again, another wish can be made, but granting the initial wish often takes so much out of the flower that it withers away before charging again.*
- *Because of this, starflowers are now very rare to find, as the people who make their wishes rarely care enough or know how to ensure the survival of the flower.*
  - o *Noting here that even though the books that Emmy quotes mention this fragility of the flower, none of them say how to prevent the starflower from dying after making a wish. When questioned, she has never seen the answer published anywhere, nor has anyone told her a way to keep one alive.*
- *How to raise your own starflowers is unknown. They have only ever been found in the wild and have never been successfully domesticated."*

Before leaving her house, Emmy showed them her moon garden. It was as beautiful as she had made it out to be. It was much smaller than the healing garden that they had seen first, but even walking onto the porch where it was kept, Brook could *feel* the difference in the atmosphere. It also helped that, with his ring on, Brook could see what each plant looked like when it was bathed in the light of the full moon. The differences were at times miraculous. He wished that he could show Trevi. Emmy was impressed by his spot-on descriptions of the moon-enhanced flowers and eyed the ring with curiosity as well as a hint of suspicion. She never said anything more about it though.

Trevi looked a bit jealous and a hint of longing had touched his eyes as he squinted and even borrowed Brook's ring for a bit to try and see the magic of the flowers for himself, but as with Emmy's hair, he just saw what was there. Emmy did promise Trevi that if he was ever around her house during a full moon, he was welcome to watch the show of the moon garden. He agreed, although tentatively, his reservations about the full moon were still in full effect.

They had left Emmy's house early in the morning, before the second sun had risen, to start their search for the starflower. The densely wooded area of Silvertree forest surrounding Emmy's house was peaceful to walk through in the pleasant weather. The silver leaves on the trees glinted with the warm hues of the rising suns. Clumps of stardust from the recent storm had gathered in shimmering piles at the base of the dark brown tree trunks after being swept there by the winds. The dew on the rich, green grass wet their feet slightly, but nourished the small, furry creatures that bounded unbothered around them while they went about their morning business.

The mountains of Alveni were a day's hike north, and they planned to scale the highest peaks to search for the starflower. Emmy had warned them that although surrounded by gentle, rolling foothills, the crags of the mountains were steep and unforgiving. A few peaks were so tall that snow fell on them even during the hottest days of summer. Many accidents happened in those mountains and some people that climbed up, never came back down.

Brook and his friends were all young and in good health, so even though the task seemed daunting, they were all up for it. Brook had briefly tried to talk them into going to the green witch's library in Waywren village that Emmy had mentioned while teaching them about the starflower instead, in his hopes to translate the text on his ring, but he had been overruled.

His heart was not against looking for the starflower anymore now that he felt more confident of its existence, so he didn't argue back...overly much. It was an unfortunate part of his nature. He admittedly did argue a *little* which ended in Emmy calling him a "pushy poodle in need of pampering." Trevi drowned out all other protests with his hearty laughter, and here they were now, trekking along a narrow, animal-made path through the solitude of the Alir wilderness en route to the mountains.

Emmy seemed to be at home in the woods. She strode softly, yet confidently, and was careful not to disturb anything too much as she passed through.

"You seem like you know this place well," Brook offered.

She nodded, "Yes, I've lived here for a while, and it is my home. I can get us up to the base of the mountains without help, but once there, I have a plan to ask for assistance."

"Assistance from whom?" Brook asked.

Emmy turned to him, and her face lit up, "Nim, of course."

"Who is Nim?" Brook asked.

"Nim is my familiar. Green witches all have their power derived from the moon, but we have different specializations. Mine involves my connection with my familiar. I can do small magic on my own, but my most powerful magic can only be done with the help of Nim. In the case of traversing the mountains, don't worry about Nim and I doing magic together to navigate through them. She is just knowledgeable about a much larger area of land than I am. She gets around a lot more being able to fly and all."

"Nim can fly? Is she a kind of bird then?" Brook asked.

"Oh, no, Nim is not a bird." Emmy shook her head, "She is a young green dragon."

Brook gasped incredulously, "You are friends with a dragon?!" He wasn't sure if he was more in awe or frightened. All the tales that he had heard about dragons while on Krael were not about them being pleasant creatures for humans to interact with. Most of the stories with dragons in them included death, destruction, cities in fiery flames, or other catastrophes.

"Yes, it is very fortunate for me that I am in tune with such a greatly magical creature. Some green witches are connected with mice, crickets, cats, or as you suggested, birds. Those creatures, although magical and majestic in their own ways, do not have the sheer power of any of the dragons."

Emmy must have noticed Brook's wary look before she continued. "You do not need to worry. Nim is not a mean creature. You may even recognize the feel of her aura when you meet her. My cards are imbued with her magic, as well as the moon's, to aid in my divinations. You can see her magic show itself in the deck, as there is an image of at least one dragon on each card."

Brook had noticed that the divination deck that Emmy had used to tell his future was covered in dragon imagery, but he had figured that it was just a themed deck of cards. Not that it was imbued with the magic of a dragon. Everything about Emmy was a whirlwind of surprises.

Trevi seized the pause in conversation as an opportunity to ask Emmy questions. "I heard from someone a long time ago that dragons had different talents based on their colors. Is that true? And, if so, what is a green dragon's specialty?"

"Yes, they do!" Emmy responded, happy to have someone interested in the specifics behind her familiar. "Dragons are indeed colored based upon their abilities. Greens are often considered 'Life Dragons' as their presence encourages plants and other animals to thrive around them. They also have a very poisonous venom that they can choose to excrete through their teeth, claws, and spines."

"Well, that poison part doesn't sound very 'life' inducing." Brook pointed out.

"Ah, but it is." Emmy smiled knowingly towards Brook, and he felt his knees weaken and his belly flop, momentarily. He still thought she was absolutely angelic, and her intelligence was also very attractive. "The dragon needs a way to protect itself and guard its own life. I assume it has acquired the poison attribute since that is the same defense mechanism that many plants use."

Trevi urged her on, "How about the other colored dragons? What are they good at?"

Emmy continued to indulge him with answers since they had nothing else to do while walking through the peaceful, wooded area. "There are red, yellow, green, blue, black, and white dragons. The first four -red, yellow, green, and blue- are purely elemental dragons. The last two -black and white- are of a more powerful nature and have soul magic as well as elemental magic."

"Reds are warmed by a natural fire inside of them. If touched, one can feel the heat that red dragons have within. The red dragon can choose to turn up or down the heat that they emanate to either comfortably warm or dangerously singe whatever touches them. They often live in cold climates since they keep themselves warm easily. These are the dragons that spit out fire breath in self-defense."

"Yellows are light dragons. They glow in the darkness and can be found in the depths of dark caves since they themselves are a light source. Similar to the way a red dragon controls the heat that they generate, a light dragon can dimly glow or brightly light up wherever they are at. They use charges of lightning as a defense mechanism."

"Blues are water dragons. They can breathe underwater and control the rains and current flows surrounding them. When angry, they are the culprits of violent storms and strong whirlpools that can sink the largest of sea vessels. When they are pleased, they are rather sociable creatures and have been seen surfing the waves in the sunlight and playing with dolphins and other sea creatures."

"Blacks are the most powerful kind of dragon. They have the greatest magic of all the beasts on Alir...and the worst attitude. Their hearts are dark and angry. They are always alone. They control the power of darkness and shadows. If you ever happen to glimpse a black dragon, my advice to you is to run away before it knows that you saw it. It doesn't take much to convince a black dragon to attack, and some just enjoy torturing other creatures for no reason. They can surround you in a bubble void of light, and you will be doomed to walk the world blindly until it pleases the dragon to release you, or it can make you feel like you are insane by plaguing your vision with shadows shaped like things that you fear. They know what you fear because they feed off of fear. Their shrill screams are a weapon that invokes your greatest fears so they can feed. It is worth noting that even though they consume your fear, they do not erase the knowledge of that fear from your memory. This means that they can continuously summon shadows of your greatest fears and eat until your mind melts."

"White dragons are sky dragons. They are light-hearted and bounce merrily across the clouds, making shapes out of them as they play. They control the winds and even sleep while flying in the skies. No one has reported seeing a live white dragon on the ground. Even though these dragons give off a jovial air, do not anger them, for as the blacks feed off of fear, white dragons feed off of dreams. If a white dragon is drawn to fight, it will eat your happiest dreams and memories, and you will never remember them again. All that will remain is a hole of true nothing. If they eat enough, you will have no more goodness left to nurture your soul, and it is pretty much guaranteed that you will turn bitter and evil for the rest of your life."

"How fascinating!" Trevi exclaimed. "I never knew

what to trust about what I had heard about dragons before now. I figured they must exist based on the plethora of stories about them, but I never truly *knew* anything about them."

"I can continue if you wish?" Emmy offered.

Trevi nodded enthusiastically, and Brook decided that maybe he should get his writing paraphernalia out to start recording this information as he had with the star flower. It could be useful to have for later, and he remembered things better when he wrote them down. As Brook was fiddling with his pack, lazily trying to get his notepad out without having to swing it over his shoulder, something slammed into him from the sky, nearly knocking him over.

"Nim!" Emmy exclaimed in pure joy as the dragon picked itself up from where it had skid onto the ground and flapped abashedly over to her shoulder where it nuzzled her face. She beamed in delight while nuzzling her back.

"Ouchy!" Brook mumbled grumpily in return trying to rub his shoulder where the small dragon had flown into him. He remembered the part about green dragons using poison and made sure that he wasn't poked by anything during the collision.

He glared over at the tiny beast on Emmy's shoulder, scrutinizing it. Nim was much smaller than he had expected. Brook had always imagined dragons as huge, lizard-like creatures with rows of sharp teeth and claws, living in cave-like dens larger than houses, and guarding hordes of treasure, not this small, fairly cute, winged creature.

Nim was indeed lizard-like. She had sharp teeth and sharp claws, but she was no larger than a house cat. She would not be able to take down a human with pure brute force, which is likely where the poison came into play. Her overlapping scales were bright emerald green, similar to the gem on his ring, and her doe-like eyes were a golden yellow with big, round, black pupils that narrowed to vertical black slits in the sunlight. Her mouth had curved up into a sweet smile and her tongue stuck out slightly as Emmy and Nim greeted each other, making the sharp teeth that he caught glances of within her small muzzle seem out of place. The spines that ran down her back and tail were flattened down so that Emmy could stroke her without fear of being stabbed.

When Emmy scratched under Nim's chin, the dragon cooed and purred contently. Those were definitely not the noises that Brook had previously associated with dragons. It was becoming very apparent that Brook's knowledge in the dragon area was lacking.

When Nim noticed Brook examining her, she sat straight up, flared out her wings, and elevated her spines. The adorable, cuddling dragon turned into a wary beast in seconds. Ah…the sinister secrets of the beautiful Alir striking again.

Emmy talked soothingly to Nim, "Shh, it's okay. These are my friends." Nim's high alert mode settled a little, but not as much as to go back to cuddling with Emmy. She sat perched on Emmy's shoulder, intently examining Brook and Trevi just as Brook had examined her.

Nim spoke inquisitively, "They are strangers. The big one has magic that I've never sensed before. It's a dark magic. The small one has magic in his ring that seems…neutral…in nature, and well…he looks a little grumpy. Are you sure they are your friends? You should surround yourself with beings who are more light-hearted."

"Like you?" Emmy responded, tickling Nim's belly.

"Of course, like me!" Nim said between giggles, and with that, Nim lightened up a bit and ran in a circle quickly around Emmy's body before stopping back on her shoulder causing Emmy to laugh too.

Trevi spoke up quickly and bowed his head apologetically, "I apologize for my darkness. My father was a demon. I do my best to control my nature, and I am trying to find a way to exorcise that part of myself to live a normal life. Brook here controls me whenever I cannot control myself."

Emmy nodded. "I suspected something of that nature from you. You give off mixed-energy vibes, but the good ones dominate. Nim here can sense magic more clearly than I can, which is why I asked her to evaluate you two in person once she got here. Please don't be ashamed. I imagine that is why you are searching for the starflower?"

Trevi nodded.

Brook interjected before Trevi could feel more awkward. "Nim ran into me!"

Emmy giggled a little. "Sorry about that! Nim is very magical, but still a baby dragon. She is a bit clumsy at times."

It was Nim's turn to feel embarrassed, and Brook was pretty sure that he saw the little dragon's green cheeks blush slightly pink. "Sorry! My flying skills are improving."

Brook waved it off. It wasn't important. He had just wanted to get the topic off of Trevi. "Are you going to get bigger as you get older since you are a baby dragon now?"

"Not too much bigger. Green dragons are the smallest of the dragons. I will always be able to sit on Emmy's shoulder, even at my largest size." Nim responded and had settled comfortably in now, preening her wings as she sat on Emmy's shoulder. "Another fifty years or so, and I will be full-grown and outgrow my adolescent clumsiness."

"Fifty years?" Brook said with a dropped jaw. "How old are you now?"

"My first hundredth birthday will come in the next few years," Nim replied nonchalantly while getting a twig out of her spines.

Brook grunted a little. He found himself feeling a bit resentful of the little dragon. How was it fair that he would lose his mind after only a mere forty living years while this 'baby' dragon would be coming out of adolescence in 150 years?

"Dragons are creatures of longevity." Emmy started to explain after seeing Brook's distraught face. "This is part of why they are so magical. It takes many years for them to be able to understand the world well enough for them to be able to fully merge with the energies that they are connected to. Once they master their magic, the magical energies themselves keep the creatures alive."

She turned her attention back to the little dragon, "I wasn't expecting to see you so early, Nim. I thought we were meeting at the foot of the mountains?"

"Change of plans. Do you remember how Siensa

accidentally invoked the rage of the black dragon that lived in the Lovlen Hills? He is making his way towards Waywren now along the base of the Alveni mountains."

"That's where we were headed!" Emmy said with widened eyes.

"Exactly. I am here early to make sure that we avoid crossing his path." Nim said dutifully.

"Shouldn't we warn father? He is almost always in Waywren nowadays."

"He knows. He had Siensa call me to make sure you were safe."

"How does he know that I was headed to the Alveni mountains?"

"He doesn't, but he knows that you live out in this general area alone and didn't want the black dragon that is looking for him and Siensa to accidentally stumble upon you and vent his rage unjustifiably. He is just looking out for you."

Brook watched the exchange between dragon and human with curiosity but didn't interrupt. He certainly didn't want to run into a black dragon now that Emmy had just told them how dangerous they were, so any information Nim was relaying could be important. He just wanted to get to the starflower and then back to the library in Waywren so that he could research the writing on his ring.

Emmy had told them yesterday that Waywren was the green witch village that she was from, and the library there was where Emmy had learned many things, including information on the starflower, while growing up. Brook hoped that by the time they went up the mountains and came back down that the black dragon issues in Waywren were cleared up. He didn't know who Siensa was, but he pitied any soul that angered one of those black dragons and wished her the best of luck.

"Let's sense his location, shall we?" Emmy said to Nim. "Then we can take a long detour around his path."

"We should be careful. If he senses us sensing him, he will likely be provoked. Especially in the particularly sour attitude that he is currently in." Nim warned.

Emmy dipped her head momentarily, but then looked up resolutely, "I know, but if we run into him, he will be even angrier, and we will have less time to escape. If we sense him from far away, and he does notice us, we will have time to run or hide. He may even be too lazy to seek us out. It sounds like he is on a mission looking for Siensa anyway. Siensa and Father will be able to handle him together. Plus, they will have the rest of the green witches at Waywren to fend him off. One black dragon against Waywren hasn't a chance. He is insane for trying."

"Siensa must have really made the black dragon angry for him to come seeking revenge like this." Nim mused.

"Yes, she did." Emmy agreed but said no more.

Brook was about to ask about the turn of events that made a black dragon angry at whoever Siensa happened to be, but Emmy silenced him with her words first. "I know what you're curious about. It's a long story; I'll tell you sometime later. We need to sense for the black dragon now before it's too late."

Brook closed his halfway-open mouth and nodded.

Emmy clutched her walking stick that had little sprigs of leaves sprouting out the top end while she and Nim closed their eyes. Brook could have sworn for a moment that he saw a silvery blue glow surround them. When Emmy opened her eyes again, she looked straight into his, for Brook hadn't taken his eyes off of her for even a moment while her eyes were closed. He saw raw fear flash across them before she was able to hide it and compose herself.

"We need to run," is all she said.

Brook looked at Trevi and then back to Emmy. She waved her arms fervently in a motion urging them to skedaddle before she gave up the encouragement and just ran between them giving them two choices: stay put in imminent danger or follow her running through the woods like their lives depended on it for the second time in only a few days.

CHAPTER 6: DECEIVING A DRAGON

$\mathcal{B}$rook fell into a bush, hands covering his face, as Emmy grabbed him mid-run to pull him inside. The bush was surprisingly hollow for how dense the outer leaves were. Trevi was already there, his large body crouched into an awkward position trying to maintain his concealment within the leaves.

"We can't outrun him," Emmy breathed heavily and spoke between gasps for air. "He knows we are here. It turns out that he was extremely close to us when we sensed for his presence. I am still glad that we reached out, seeing as he would have crossed our path anyway. We were right in between him and Waywren."

She looked to Nim, "Ready?"

"Always," Nim responded.

Silvery blue wisps surrounded them as Emmy explained what they were doing. "We are creating a dense, thorny thicket atop swampy grounds surrounding our current location. That terrain will be a great nuisance for the black dragon to fumble through. Considering that he has no quarrel with us, I am hoping that his general laziness will get the better of him, and he will choose to go around the thicket so that he can reach Waywren faster."

"Why can't you use your moony-ness and dragon-ness combined to create a forcefield that he cannot penetrate? Or make us invisible to him?" Brook asked.

"As I said before," Emmy calmly explained, "Black dragons are the most powerful creatures on Alir. I am no match with my green dragon against him. If he chooses to fight us, we will likely not survive, and he will be able to see through any defenses that we put up. We need to make ourselves look as un-enticing as possible in his eyes. It's our only hope."

Brook sat still, wedged in between Trevi and Emmy. None of them spoke anymore since they all seemed to be holding their breath in anticipation of what the black dragon would choose to do. The great beast came into view through the forest. First in glimpses through the trees, and then Brook could see his face. This was a beast to cower before. Its size dwarfed any living creature that Brook had seen in the past. He stepped on small trees as though they were mere sticks to make his way through the forest. His scales were darker than a moonless midnight sky and shined with a mirror-like reflection as the sunlight hit them through the trees. This was a dragon befitting of the terrors, descriptions, and stories that Brook had heard.

Two horns twirled out of his head with blood-red swirls that accented his bright red eyes that were searching the area. His massive, yellow-stained, curved teeth that hung out of his mouth matched his equally massive claws that sunk into the forest floor with each step that he took. He had no wings to fly, but that seemed like a minor inconvenience based on the magnificence of his strongly muscled and scale-shielded body.

He stopped when one of his feet sunk into the swampy lands that Emmy and Nim had created. It made a loud sucking noise as he drew it back out onto the solid ground and shook off the mud in irritation. His long neck swerved while his eyes swept the area, now covered in a thorny thicket, before stopping on the little set of bushes that they were hiding in.

"He can sense us here. Don't do anything unexpected to draw his rage." Emmy warned.

The dragon took his eyes off of them and looked in another direction, towards Waywren, considering.

"It's working!" Trevi said excitedly.

"That's my hope," Emmy said, not taking her eyes off of the deciding dragon. "Stay calm. Stay positive. If we are too afraid, he may stop to snack on our fear after sensing how delicious it is."

After a few intense minutes, the black dragon took a step towards the non-swampy area that led in the direction of Waywren. The group let out a sigh of relief, but it was a moment too soon. Brook could have sworn that he saw the corner of the black dragon's mouth twitch upwards in amusement before turning his head up to the skies and letting out a shrill, terrifying scream. Shadows emerged, squirming from the scream itself, and descended onto their little bush hideout.

"No," Emmy whispered. Holding onto where her heart was beating in her chest. She turned to the boys, "Do not succumb. Think happy thoughts. Combat the fears. Do not indulge his snacking desires, or he may not stop!"

Brook heard her, but he couldn't immediately come up with any good thoughts. He felt the burden of his short life crash down upon him. He relived the night that he watched his father's mind disappear. He had known what day it would happen, and they had spent it together. Brook was in denial the whole day as his father gave him any last pointers that he could to help in finding a solution to the curse that plagued both of them. In the evening, before bed, his father had held both of Brook's hands, staring into his eyes. He had told Brook that he had faith in him and that he should not lose hope. He assured Brook that they were close to finding the answer. He placed the ring on Brook's hand and patted it lovingly. His father had held Brook's gaze as his mind left his body. Brook remembered the intensity of his eyes softening into nothing, and he thought that he saw some blackish-grey color swirl away from his father's head and out of a nearby window. Brook had lost hold of himself for a few days afterward. Crying and hiding in his house with the fear of when he would succumb to the same fate as his father. Trevi had finally rescued Brook from himself, but the black dragon's magic wouldn't let him think of that.

Brook imagined what it would be like to fail in his search to understand his cursed ring and to join all of his father's fathers before him in their uncurable madness. He imagined leaving Trevi alone to face the horrors of his inner demon. He imagined Trevi turning on him in his demonic form and being unable to contain his demonic rage, and then someone else slaying his one true friend in the world because Brook had not been good enough.

Then he saw Emmy looking at him, urging him with her eyes to combat the fear and darkness. He had to try. It took tremendous effort, and there seemed to be a wall in his mind that he had to tediously extract each thought through before thinking about it. He recalled the previous day when he had thought he had met an angel. He recalled how special he had felt when his ring allowed him to see the moon's magic. The shadows around him dispelled slightly.

He recalled when he had first met Trevi as a young boy being bullied by some town kids for being a 'demon'. Trevi had unleashed his inner demon when the kids turned their meanness towards an innocent bystander who happened to be walking close to them, pushing her down for no reason, and then laughing. He had contained Trevi then, beating back his demon with the sword techniques that he had learned from his father. When Trevi had turned back into his fully human form, he had thanked Brook. The other bully kids and the girl that Trevi had tried to protect had all run off by that time, and no one bothered either of them face-to-face after that. That's when Brook's father had taken Trevi in, and they became brothers.

The shadows no longer plagued Brook, and he turned his attention to Trevi. It was too late. The fears that Trevi had seen must have been too much for him. Brook could see the veins expanding in his upper back as it arched upward, jutting his head forward. His eyes were already pure red, like those of the dragon, and a short muzzle with sharpened teeth expanded from his white and wolf-like head. His skin steeled into a tough, red and black coating, and pointed claws extracted from his fingers. He was no longer Trevi.

"Hide from his sight. I will bring him back." Brook said to Emmy. She grew a green curtain of leaves between them as Trevi finished his transformation. To Brook's surprise, the demon howled and then leaped out towards the dragon!

Brook leaped after him instinctively, sword in hand.

"He won't be able to fight it!" Emmy yelled from the bushes.

Brook knew she was right, but he couldn't let Trevi be out here alone with the dragon. His feet were sucked into the ground, and thorns tore at his clothes as he tried to run after Trevi. Trevi's demonic feet were wider and longer than human's feet, which allowed him to stay atop the sucking mud long enough for him to run quickly towards the dragon with his thickened skin protecting him from the thorns.

The dragon seemed even more amused by this turn of events. Brook was stuck. Stuck in the mud, unable to help his friend. He was living one of his worst fears. He watched as Trevi tried slashing at the scales of the dragon with his claws, but they were impenetrable. He tried to climb up the dragon, but it just pawed at him with its giant front claws. The demon snarled before the dragon whipped its tail at him and dangled it just out of the demon's reach on the ground, wiggling it ever so slightly. The demon lunged for it in an attack, and the dragon pulled it away at the last second, swiping him with a giant foreclaw in punishment. The dragon was playing with him like a cat does with a toy.

A gruesome smile was spread across the beast's face as the demon tried his hardest to take down the mighty dragon. Brook hated the dragon for toying with Trevi, but he also knew that as long as it wasn't fighting back, then Trevi still had a chance. Brook kept slowly making his way towards the fruitless battle and felt the ground solidify more and saw the thorns retract. Emmy was draining the swamp and changing it back to the forest floor.

He ran to the battle, not sure what he could do to help. The demon looked in his direction momentarily and growled. Brook knew that demon Trevi fought all things in demonic form. He did not distinguish between friend and foe. Keeping that in mind, Brook tried to engage the dragon in other ways, far away from Trevi. His sword was useless against the dragon's hard scales, and the force with which the dragon's foreclaws hit him knocked him over, whereas at least Trevi's demonic form had remained standing. Brook didn't know how they were going to get out of this.

Something suddenly hit the black dragon from above. It was a tail. A pearly white, scaled tail. A sky dragon descended onto the black dragon by latching its claws onto its back. Its massive, white wings spread out with impressive plumage as it crashed through the forest canopy. It was about the same size as the black dragon, but instead of being built with four paws easily accessing the ground, like the black and green dragons, this dragon was snake-like with four short legs that ended in claws made for grasping tall and large tree branches. The sky dragon took a bite of the black dragon's neck behind its horns. The black dragon screamed and shadows descended upon the white dragon. The bite had not penetrated the scales completely, but it had caused the blood of the assaulted black dragon to be spilled. The white dragon took off, flying low, and the black dragon took chase, leaving the pitiful human toys behind.

With the black dragon gone, Trevi turned his rage onto Brook who began to parry his demonic strikes with his sword. This was now returning to a situation that Brook could handle. Brook looked over his shoulder and saw Emmy, as well as some other people that Brook didn't recognize, starting to gather around them. Trevi made a lunge for Emmy who deftly evaded the strike. Brook jumped in front of her and continued to bash down on demonic Trevi's assault. Time was the only thing that healed Trevi's condition, and Brook was an able swordsman willing to take all the time his friend needed to return to normal.

Before Trevi could return, a mass of vines tied demonic Trevi down, suppressing his fight. The demon fought and screamed at the vines entangling him. Tearing at them to escape, but as fast as he could tear the vines down, more appeared. This went on for some time before Brook saw the red light of his eyes deaden. The blue started to return. Then his back unhunched, and his claws retracted. His skin returned to a normal human color instead of being tinted with red and black splotches.

"Welcome back, friend," Brook said as he sheathed his sword and walked towards him. Trevi's shirt and pants were torn from the transformation but still hung onto him. He had tears in his eyes like he always did after transforming. Brook wasn't sure if it was physical or mental pain that caused them. He just knew that Trevi truly hated his demonic form.

"It's okay, Trevi. You didn't hurt anyone. The black

dragon got to you with his shadows. It'll be all right." Brook reassured the toppled man by reaching through the vines and resting a comforting hand on Trevi's shoulder.

Trevi grabbed his hand and said, "Thank you, again, brother."

Brook turned to Emmy and saw two other men standing beside her. He called back to them, "You can let him out now. He is back to normal!"

They were conversing in tones too low for Brook to hear, but he wasn't going to leave Trevi's side. One of the men came to Brook instead.

"Greetings, Brook. I am the elder from Waywren village. I am also Emmy's father. After seeing Trevi attack my daughter and upon council from the village shaman, I cannot free your friend. He must come back with us and face judgment."

"But we need to search for the starflower!" Brook protested.

The village elder raised a hand quieting him. Emmy has told me all of your plans. You will have to put them on hold or go without Trevi. You are free to go, but your friend will be taken back to Waywren with us."

"What about the black dragon? Wasn't he going to attack Waywren?"

"Siensa will keep him distracted until she brings him to a group of green witches who will neutralize or scare him off. It is, after all, Siensa who he was after."

Brook thought for a moment. It all made sense to him now. "So Siensa is your familiar, just as Nim is Emmy's familiar? It would make sense that father and daughter would have the same types of talents."

"You are smart enough, Brook, but enough talk for now. Will you be coming with us to Waywren?"

Yesterday, he had been arguing with Emmy and Trevi to go straight to Waywren so he could scour the library there, but now that he was directly invited by the village elder, Brook felt uneasy and wanted to go about their original plans of finding the starflower in the Alveni mountains first. It wasn't the village elder that made him uneasy. He looked like a kind, older gentleman with creases around his eyes from the stress and responsibilities of his leadership position. It was the circumstances, and maybe a little of that creepy shaman guy standing too close to Emmy for Brook's liking. Brook thought he saw a light black mist swirling around the places where the shaman's skin was exposed from beneath the hooded cloak drooping over his head to hide his face, but it could have been a trick of the light and shadows in the forest.

"Yes, I will come with you. Is Emmy coming?"

"Yes, she will come with us, too. She said that she would do the same as whatever you decided to do. I'll let her know." The village elder said before starting to make his way back to where the shaman and Emmy stood.

"Wait!" Brook called before he got too far.

The elder stopped, waiting for Brook to continue, but not turning around to face him.

"Who is that next to Emmy?" Brook asked. "He, uh, gives me a bad feeling."

"Do not worry about him. He has been the Waywren village shaman for many years. His loyalty to the green witches is unquestionable, regardless of his appearance." With that, the elder continued back towards Emmy and the shaman.

Brook was not happy about this situation. He turned back to Trevi who looked at him with sad eyes. "I'm sorry, Brook. I didn't mean to."

"I know, Trevi. It's not your fault. We will get out of this, somehow. We always do." Brook reassured his friend even though he wasn't so sure that he felt reassured himself.

CHAPTER 7: WITCHES OF WAYWREN

Brook sat comfortably on a wooden stool carved into the shape of a squirrel. His rump was on top of its fluffy, up-curled tail, as he sat outside the green witch guest hut within the village elder's clearing that he was given for the night. He had recently awoken from a well-needed sleep in a bed made of soft, velvety leaves that had a sweet, lavender-like scent to them. That scent combined with the texture of the leaves had helped lull him into a deep and restful sleep unlike any that he remembered experiencing in years. It made Brook wonder if there had been some kind of magic imbued into the bed itself.

The hike to Waywren the days before had been relatively uneventful. The elder and the shaman had made Trevi walk between them along the way to be kept 'contained.' Brook had been able to talk them out of tying his arms together for the walk, but Trevi seemed pretty amenable to whatever the green witches wanted to do to punish him since he knew that he had indeed turned into a demon in front of them, and he could remember lunging at Emmy when he couldn't control himself. Trevi had profusely apologized, but he knew that he couldn't guarantee that it wouldn't happen again unless they could exorcize his demonic nature once and for all.

For what it was worth, the elder and shaman had listened to Trevi's plea and said that they would think about if any green witch magic could be used to help in his exorcism. They had even mentioned looking through the library at Waywren. This news had brought a merry bounce into Trevi's steps, even though he was being held captive. Brook's spirits were lifted as well since he would now have plenty of excuses to go through the books in the library.

On their trip, Emmy had also regaled them with the story of how Siensa angered the black dragon which had revealed some of the petty pride that existed within the dark hearts of the black dragons. Thinking back on the story now, Brook couldn't help but smile as he imagined the way that Emmy had animatedly moved about as she told the tale that began the feud of the black and white dragons. She had twirled and growled and pounced and made entertaining facial expressions to add flavor to her story that made it memorable to him.

Her voice played itself back in his mind, "Sky dragons are a whimsical lot, and the world is their playground. They enjoy the freedom of the boundless skies, a realm that they alone can visit at staggering heights. Siensa has a bit of an artistic streak for a dragon and is particularly fond of making shapes in the clouds as she flies through them. The sky is her canvas, the clouds her paints, and her body the paintbrush as she twists and twirls and flourishes the clouds' vapor droplets into artistic masterpieces. She is well-known amongst the green witches and many keep an eye up to the skies in hopes to catch a glimpse of her unique and magnificent artwork."

"Siensa had been doodling around the same area of the sky for a few weeks. This was odd for her, as she usually would fly elsewhere after making her doodles, but the whims of sky dragons are hard to characterize, and she doesn't even know why she does the things that she does other than they tickled her fancy at the time. This area of the sky happened to be over the lair of the black dragon, Cauron. Cauron had a bit of a superstitious streak, and he watched those clouds change shape every day, but never happened to examine them while Siensa was creating the shapes."

"Black dragons may be the most powerful creatures alive, but they are still sentient beings who are capable of emotions: including fear. If there is a creature that abhors fear more than any other, it is ironically the black dragon. They do not appreciate when their own tactics are used against them, and fear is their primary weapon. Cauron had believed that the world was coming to an end and that this was being signaled by the frequent changes of the clouds above him into prominent shapes. This had caused him to go into hiding and to begin hoarding all the necessities that he would require for survival inside his caves."

"One day, he looked up into the clouds to see what they were currently heralding, and he finally saw Siensa swooping around, concentrating on her latest artwork. He was livid. The shrill shadow screech that he let out in anguish spread his cursed fear for miles onto unsuspecting victims. Tendrils even reached

Siensa in the skies, who looked down upon the world below to see the enraged black dragon throwing his temper tantrum. Cauron turned his fear into a rage and now channels it towards seeking revenge upon Siensa."

The sound of a smile in Emmy's real voice interrupted the one in Brook's mind, "Dallying in daydreams is delightful, isn't it?"

Brook had quite the silly, absent-minded smile on his face when she found him, and he shook his head to bring his brain back to where his physical body was before responding. "Yes, of course. Especially when they are pleasant ones."

"Well, maybe you can tell me about them on the way to the library? I'd love to hear them."

Brook could feel his cheeks redden in embarrassment. There was no way that he could tell her that he had been daydreaming about her. "Maybe another time. I was just sorting through some thoughts, trying to make sense of them." He turned his head, looking slightly down and away from her, as he rubbed the back of his head hoping she hadn't seen the color of his hot cheeks.

"Well, you can make lots of cents sharing those thoughts, one day, as I have pennies to part with!" Emmy said encouragingly before waving for him to follow her with a slight skip in her step.

Brook stood up and let the early light of the day warm his face as he stretched before following Emmy through the maze of Waywren to the library. Waywren was built in clumps of forest clearings. The larger tree's encircling the clearings let in light through their leaves high above so as not to engulf the village clusters in shadows. The morning light shined upon the little hemispherical huts built with bendy sticks for the base structure and covered with large, thick leaves dotting the various clearings. This was the general style of houses in Waywren. Many wooden carvings were used as benches, tables, and decorations scattered around the outsides of the huts, adding hints of character to the similar-looking houses.

Different clearings had different numbers of houses and each had unique names. For instance, Brook had stayed in "Elder's Clearing" last night, they were currently walking through "Sunrise Clearing", and the library was located in "Reading Clearing." There were trails between the clearings that could be traversed giving each clump of houses a semblance of privacy from the other clumps of houses.

It was early enough in the morning that not many of Waywren's occupants were outside, yet. Either that or the presence of the newcomers in their village was making the villagers wary. Brook squinted purposefully at one of the windows of a nearby hut in a clearing that they were passing through and saw a wooden shutter quickly swing shut. Yupp; thought confirmed. The green witches were avoiding him. Brook didn't want to scare these people, so he tried to make it obvious that his attention was elsewhere by talking to Emmy. He had good questions for her anyway.

"Can you tell me a bit about your local shaman? He kinda creeps me out a little."

"Morag? Hmm. Well, he has been around here for as long as anyone remembers. He has had an extremely long lifetime and knows many things. He generally keeps to himself, but the village elders have always heeded his counsel and kept him close. They find his advice useful in many things from menial weather predictions to the heralding of catastrophic and lifestyle-altering events."

"Elders? As in, plural?" Brook inquired with surprise. "He has outlived more than one village elder?"

"Yes, I believe so." Emmy nodded.

"Doesn't that mean he has pretty much run this village for however long he has lived?" Brook asked with a healthy dose of suspicion.

"He claims that he wants nothing to do with leadership and only wishes to advise others who would shoulder that burden," Emmy replied calmly as though that was a fact so obvious that it was never disputed.

Brook noticed a faint wisp of black mists swirling away from Emmy's head. "Don't you ever wonder about Morag? It just seems suspicious to just trust someone like that so implicitly without thinking more about it."

Emmy didn't respond immediately. Seemingly, taking that moment to think about it. "I have thought about it. Suspicions came to me while I have been living outside the village in my own house, but now that I've returned to Waywren, I have this strange feeling that I need not worry or think too much about it any longer. Waywren has lived in peace and prosperity for as long as we can remember. We strive to keep it a safe place for all green witches who aspire to come here."

Emmy stopped walking for a moment and

breathed heavily inwards, holding it for a few seconds before blowing it out in a slow and controlled fashion. A hint of silvery blue mist attempted to get into her head, but a black vapor shielded it away.

"What are you doing?" Brook asked.

"Clearing my mind with the help of moon magic to help me to see more clearly that which is strangely obscured," Emmy explained.

"Well, if moon magic is silvery blue, then it can't get into your head because of that other black misty stuff surrounding it," Brook said while waving his hands around in amorphous circles about her head.

"Uh, what?" Emmy curled her nose up and squinted an eye signaling her confusion.

"You're the magicky one, don't you know what I mean? I certainly have no clue. I'm just telling you what I see." Brook shrugged helplessly.

Wide-eyed in surprise, Emmy pulled her divination deck out of her bag and held it up for Brook to see. "Do you see anything surrounding these cards?" She asked insistently.

"No, not right now."

"How about now?" Emmy dropped to the ground, cross-legged, and started playing the cards in front of her as she did when telling Brook's future.

"Yes, some silvery blue mist, again," Brook said as he cocked his head to the side and wondered what or whose future she was divining.

Emmy finished her card layout without saying anything and took in what she saw there before turning to look up at Brook. She gathered her cards and stuck out her arm to him, which he took and helped her back to her feet.

She faced Brook, put both her hands on his shoulders, and searched his eyes before hugging him close.

Brook melted. He was all sorts of tingly and confused in the grasp of his angel. She smelled and felt so wonderful that close to him. He eventually remembered that when being hugged you should probably hug that person back, so he put his arms gently around her body in return.

Emmy giggled a little, standing slightly on her toes, bringing her lips close to one of his ears. Her warm breath blowing softly on his ear was almost one sensation too many for Brook to bear as she whispered something to him. "Shh… I'm pretty sure that you can see moon magic from what you've told me. I don't want others listening in on us to hear, so I hugged you to tell you in secret. I think you can not only see normal moon magic, but dark moon magic as well. Follow my lead."

And as quickly as she had swept him up into an unannounced hug, she released him and grabbed his hand, running off towards the woods, looking back at him every so often with little laughs and stunning smiles. This left Brook no choice but to trot along behind her with a bemused look plastered on his face, smiling even more each time she looked back at him. Brook figured that the image that they were leaving the green witches of Waywren with was one of two lovebirds flitting away to be alone in the woods. He only hoped Emmy's father wasn't the kind to get over-protective in an instance like this. He hoped Emmy knew what she was doing.

Once Emmy finally stopped their flight, they were

deep in the woods. She checked the areas around them and sat Brook down next to her on a large, fallen log. "We should be safe here to talk for a little bit. Can you tell me exactly what you see and when?"

"Sure," Brook said. "Right now, I see you emitting wisps of silvery blue mists. Every so often, I catch a glimpse of it in a dome around us."

Emmy nodded, "I am constructing a small sound barrier around us with my moon magic. And now, what do you see?"

The mists now returned to swirling around Emmy's head but were blocked by the black mists that he saw before. He described that as best as he could to Emmy. "The silvery blue mist is surrounding your head and 'poking' at a shell of black mists that will not let it enter. I do not see the black mist unless the silvery blue mist is interacting with it."

"Interesting," Emmy mused. "I think someone has used dark moon magic on the people of Waywren to prevent us from thinking about certain things. One of those things happens to be Morag's long lifespan and his involvement with the village elders. Even just speaking to you about it now, I get this reassuring feeling that it's all fine and as it should be, and that there is no reason for me to be spending any effort thinking along these lines. But I distinctly remember being suspicious about this for…reasons…when I was at my house, far from here."

Emmy paused for a moment, looking as though she was deep in thought. Brook saw tendrils of the blue mist pricking holes into the dark mist.

"If it helps, I remember seeing dark mists around Morag when I first met him. That was part of what made him seem eerie, to me."

The black mists thickened over Emmy's head as it seemingly took her much effort to say the next words, "Morag uses dark moon magic?"

Her hand went to her forehead in a futile attempt to do something about the mental blockage, but the mists were more powerful than a simple hand. She spoke again, "My mother, Auraline, left Waywren after speaking her suspicions on this matter you propose. I've not seen her since. She was part of why I felt compelled to leave Waywren and live on my own. I guess, a part of me hoped that I would find her, or she would find me, if I left. I wonder where she has gone. I wonder if this is all related."

Emmy sighed, "I wish I could think straight right now. We need to get far away from here so I can sort through this properly. Distance seems to weaken the dark magic's hold on me. This curse must have been put on the residents long ago, since you, as a newcomer, are not being affected by it."

Brook saw the light moon mist and dark moon mist beginning to fight furiously above her head. He scooted over closer to her and wrapped a hesitant arm around her shoulders. That shouldn't be too scary for him since she had just hugged him, but his stomach was flopping in a distracting manner anyway. She huddled in closer to him as the mists battled above her head.

"We need to rescue Trevi before we go." Brook insisted, immediately feeling guilty that he mentioned that when she was feeling like this.

"Obviously! I'd have it no other way." She agreed without the slightest hesitation. That made Brook feel better about her, and he pulled her closer. Emmy reached towards his hand with the ring on it but stopped when a thought hit her before taking his hand in hers to hold.

She asked softly, "May I take it off? I want to see if your ability to see moon magic is tied to the ring, like the way you could see the moon garden blooms at home."

Brook nodded and let her remove the ring from his right hand since his left arm was around her side in a comforting manner.

"They're gone now," Brook said after the ring had been removed. Brook felt no different, but the colorful mists had disappeared from his vision.

"You try it on, and tell me if you can see anything." Brook offered.

Emmy hesitated with the ring slightly over her finger before putting it onto her hand and looking around. "I...I don't see anything different."

"Trevi couldn't either when he tried," Brook reassured her.

"This ring...and you...are something special. We should find out as much as we can about your connections." Emmy murmured as she removed the ring from her slender finger, and gingerly slid it back onto Brook's larger one. Her delicate touch was divine, and Brook soaked it in. Once the ring was back on, he saw the moon mists return to his vision.

"Believe me," Brook said emphatically, "There is nothing more I'd rather do. I've spent my entire lifetime trying to figure it out, and so have my ancestors. Although, this 'seeing' of moon magic is a new discovery. Heck, I didn't even know moon magic existed until I met you."

"Well, now you have the help of a clever, green witch to unravel the ring's secrets. So, surely, you cannot fail." Emmy said playfully bringing levity to the sincere moment. They leaned closer to each other while sitting on the log deep in the forest. They sat in the silence and comfort of each other's company for a little while, taking in the peace and beauty of the forest around them.

CHAPTER 8: A DEMONIC DELVE

$\mathcal{T}$revi was cold. He knew if he let the demon control him that he would be warm again, but he couldn't let himself succumb to that. He had to let that temptation out of his mind as he shivered in the corner of his prison. That demon was what got him into this predicament in the first place. He would have never guessed that the green witches that he hiked here with would have kept such a dank and disgusting place. They seemed so fresh and kind and willing to help him overcome his inner demon. Then they arrived at Waywren, and everything changed. The elder went off to his clearing, and the shaman, Morag, brought him down underground into this prison that he was starting to think they never intended to release him from.

The air smelled as if the same molecules had been circulating down here for years and that fresh air was never bestowed upon the inmates. Water dripped periodically from the ceiling which made the stuffy, cold room damp and even more uncomfortable. A bed had been carved out of the rock and dirt walls for Trevi to lay on when needed, but it was almost preferable to stand with all the rocky knobs poking through and tiny bugs rooting around it.

Through the metal bars of his cell, he could see a wall of dirt across the walkway. If he angled himself appropriately, he could tell that there was a cell diagonal from his across the walkway, but he could not see more into it than the front corner. The witches must not have wanted the prisoners to see each other. He thought about calling down the hallway to see if anyone answered, but thought better of it. He wasn't sure what else was being kept down here.

The elder had said that they would hold his trial in five days and that he would only be held in the dungeons until then. Emmy had protested saying that she dropped all charges since she was the one that he attacked, but Morag and the elder had consulted and deemed the demon a danger to more than just Emmy, so therefore he needed to undergo a trial by the council of the green witches. Brook and Emmy had reassured him that they would scour the library for a way to heal Trevi in the meantime, and they did their best to convince him that they would release him easily after the trial.

Trevi was beginning to doubt this very much. When the shaman had brought him down here, he had passed by the most disturbing of sights. One of those sights was what he could best describe as a laboratory. There had been preserved bodies of various races of a myriad of creatures held in transparent glass coffins of liquid. Beakers and tubes of various colored liquids snaked around the room and into those coffins. Strange ingredients in jars sat in lines along the shelves on the walls. And the smell… pew! Trevi had held his breath as much as he could when they had walked through there, and still, the stench leaked into his senses.

Over the last couple of days, he had been listening through the walls of his cell in the direction of that laboratory. There were odd chants, screams, and conversations that made no sense. He had recently decided that the conversations had made no sense because they were the shaman, Morag, talking to himself. He only heard bits and pieces, but he seemed interested in adding demon blood to his 'new moon' ritual. Whatever that was. That was particularly disturbing to Trevi since he was pretty sure that the likelihood of Morag knowing another demon beyond himself was quite low.

Morag would come by with food three times a day, and Trevi easily knew when that was by the squeal of the unoiled door, followed by the *thunk, thunk, thunk* of Morag's tall, ancient-looking, wooden staff on the floor. The nuts that were tied to the knotted top made noises similar to the plinks of raindrops on a pond's surface when the staff swayed as he walked, and that was, sadly, the most comforting noise that Trevi heard in this wretched place. He heard the plinking now as midday meal time approached, and Trevi felt his belly rumble in anticipation but his body tremble in fear.

Morag went straight to Trevi's cell, neglecting any other stops along the way for other prisoners, so it wasn't long before what looked like a human-less cloak peered at Trevi through the bars. Trevi had yet to see Morag's face since it was always covered by the shadows created by the folds of his dense fabric cloak, but Morag's voice crackled with ancient hoarseness any time that he spoke and was distinct enough from any other voice that Trevi had heard. This made Trevi confident that it was the same person coming for each visit.

An old, weathered hand with skin folds almost as dense as the ones in his cloak reached into the iron bars of Trevi's cell with a small plate of unappetizing food that had proven minorly nourishing in the past. Just enough to cut the edge off of Trevi's hunger pangs. Trevi reached forward to grab the plate, as he had always done before, but this time, quicker than a snake lashing out to grab its victim, Morag's other hand slid through the cell bars and stabbed Trevi's arm with a needle attached to a vial and pumped an unknown liquid into his veins.

Trevi yelped in a dog-like fashion at the unexpected turn of events, pulling his hand back from the meal being offered. The plate of food dropped to the floor with the harsh clang and clatter of metal on stone. The small amount of food on it was strewn across the cell floor haphazardly. Trevi felt the flow of poison through his arm's veins. It stung, then it burned, and then it scorched his insides as he felt the toxin spread up from his arm and into his torso, eventually consuming his entire body.

Screams of agony escaped Trevi's mouth as his hands grasped his head as if they could hold in what was about to happen. He fell to the floor on his knees, fighting the demon within him threatening to swell up to the surface. What was this poison? Was it calling upon his inner demon? Trevi was confused since he had not gotten emotional enough about the ambush with the needle to warrant his usual demonic transformation.

Almost as though Morag had heard his thoughts, he encouraged the transformation, "Yes. Yes. Come out my pretty little demon. Let your true self emerge from the weak human's body that you possess. No need to let him keep you trapped anymore. You are free to do your own bidding. Shed this puny human skin for your true might and grandeur!"

Human Trevi was still fighting the demon as he looked up from his kneeling position on the ground into Morag's hood. He saw the most disconcerting glow coming from what must have been Morag's eyes. If the color of a shadow could glow upon a black background, that would be the best way that Trevi could explain the eyes that he saw within the folds of the cloak. They were anything but normal. Almost…undead.

Something was different about this demon transformation that he was experiencing when compared to his others. It was abnormal as it was not triggered by Trevi's feelings, but by the vile vial of poison that Morag had administered. Trevi was still losing the battle, standard transformation or not. He saw his arm that had been punctured by the needle transform first into its hard carapace form, blotched with red and black. He felt the rest of the transformation follow as his neck and back bent upwards and forward in a completely unnatural fashion before finishing out his demonic snout and teeth. It didn't hurt Trevi physically, but mentally it crushed him because he knew that his mind would be the last to succumb to the demonic form. As the demonic fog began to cloud his mind, he looked one last time into Morag's hood, and if glowing, shadow eyes could hint at a smile, these did.

"Good, little demon," Morag cooed. "I can't wait to see how demonic blood strengthens my collection of souls." And with that, Morag turned and walked away, returning down the hallway of cells. Demonic Trevi was enraged as he grabbed the metal cell bars with his clawed hands and tried to bend them as he unleashed a ravaging roar. Morag's response was the unbothered closing of the door to the dungeon as he walked out. That was the last straw for demonic Trevi who turned around and kicked the cell door with his haunches. The door broke open from the pure strength that coursed through a demon's kick. One bottom hinge was still connected as the door fell to the floor as if to show the world that it had tried its hardest. Blinded by anger, demonic Trevi reached the prison door that Morag had recently shut and punched it down off both its hinges, leaving an indent of his demonic fist in the metal as a calling card.

Once Trevi had broken down the door and didn't immediately see Morag to attack. He realized something. Human Trevi's mind was not completely gone. At first, it was a tiny whisper. Then it became clearer as demon Trevi focused his mind on it. Through gritted teeth and growls. Trevi halted his rampage as he unfurled and furled his fists to try and beat down the normally overwhelming rage. To his surprise, it was working. The anger was still there, but it was almost as if Trevi had a dual mind now. He tried with all his might to quell the rest of the anger, but no matter what he did something still brewed deep in his soul, and his body refused to change back to human.

After a few attempts, Trevi finally took a look around the room that he was in. It was the laboratory that he had passed through on the way to the dungeon with Morag the first day that he was brought here. Through his demonic eyes, he could see what he could not as a human: dark moon magic. He knew it for what it was after hearing it explained by Emmy. Dark swirls of mist clung to the apparatuses in the room and the jars on the shelves. The disconcerting clear liquid coffins that had disturbed him before allowed for the dark swirls to shine through the preserving liquid as it writhed its way around the prisoners within. An ancient-looking book with an old leather binding lay open on the wooden table in the center of the room as if it had been recent reading material. A spell book, perhaps?

There were two doors leading from this room. One was the door that Trevi had been led down here through. That one should have been his goal, but the darkness that seeped through the crack beneath the other door called to him. While he was here and unable to change from his demonic form, he should look and see what was inside. He could protect himself in this form, and he could see moon magic. At least the dark kind. That was sure to give him an advantage as he snooped around the shaman's place.

As careful as he could be with his long, demonic claws, Trevi worked the handle to the door into the new room. It was unlocked. When he stepped in, an atrocious smell assaulted his enhanced senses which would have made a human stomach empty itself, but not that of a demon. Trevi merely took a few sniffs and noted it for recognition later, as a dog would have.

The darkness that swirled in this room was countered by a bright array of hazy light balls lined up in an orderly fashion along the extra tall cylindrical walls of the room. There was a strand of darkness tethering each light ball to a larger and darker hazy light ball in the center of the room creating a web of misty threads that didn't exist in the physical world. Trevi could walk through them, and they would snap back into the intricate web that they had been originally woven into as soon as he passed through.

This was some deep, dark moon magic. One of the bright light balls along the wall called to Trevi. It seemed familiar, in a way, to him. As he approached it, the familiarity grew and became recognizable. A knot of hope formed in his stomach, almost quenching his demonic form, but not quite.

"Father," he whispered to the ball of light but earned no response. He delicately touched the little ball of light with the very tip of his clawed finger, and his mind was shown the memories of the man he considered his father. He saw the way this soul had taken him in as a child, even though they shared no blood. He saw the way it had toiled away to solve the mystery of the forty-year curse, the same curse that plagued Brook. He saw many other personal and touching memories that he recognized, too. This was undoubtedly the soul of Brook's father. The other little lights aligned so perfectly along the edges of the shelves in the room must have been the souls of Brook's ancestors, and maybe others, that Morag had stolen for himself to indulge upon.

Trevi was about to ask himself why, but on the pedestal holding up the ominous, dark ball in the center of the room, which must have been Morag's dark soul, there was creepy writing etched in wisps of dark moon magic: ETERNAL LIFE.

Trevi needed to get Brook this information quickly. He realized now that Morag never intended to let him survive the trial. Trevi was going to become one of the souls that he sucked the life out from after they condemned him if there was even going to be a trial. The demonic fury fired up inside Trevi again as he blasted through the remaining doors until he was free from the confines of Morag's laboratory in the brilliant afternoon sun.

It was pure pandemonium. The townsfolk of Waywren who saw Trevi's demon screamed and ran, dropping whatever they were holding and grabbing small children to pull them away from his proximity. It was then that Trevi realized that he had made a minor miscalculation. He was still a demon and a pretty terrifying one that had attacked a powerful black dragon and the village elder's daughter a few days past. Bursting out of his jail confines at midday in this demonic form may not have been one of his better decisions.

He tried to dim the anger enough to transform back into his human form again but failed. The panic in the town surrounding him was escalating. When he looked around and couldn't find Brook or Emmy immediately, he knew that he had to run away from this place. He was scaring people for no reason, Morag would be back for his demonic soul specimen, and Emmy's father was a strong green witch elder with a white dragon familiar who would want to protect his town. Trevi would have to run deep into the woods until this demonic episode timed out and would then attempt to locate Brook. Thankfully, this time, he was mostly in control of the demon, even though he didn't fully understand why.

CHAPTER 9: DISPELLING THE BEAUTY OF BUTTERFLIES

*T*he wind played with a few of Brook's curls as he sat on the large, fallen log in the secluded wooded clearing that he and Emmy returned to daily to discuss their findings from town and the library. Emmy was humming to herself while a few brightly colored butterflies fluttered in circles around her, lightly bouncing in the shifting directions of the wind. She was examining a sweet-smelling flower growing from a hollow in the trunk of a tree to which the butterflies had been drawn. A small mechanism was in her hand that she used to extract the nectar without harming the flower itself. Brook loved watching her work. Something about the way she exuded joy and delicacy as she carried on with her day-to-day life made him feel comforted and more happy than usual. He caught himself smiling in her direction, unnoticed by her absorption in work, before his mind changed paths toward his usual dreary thoughts.

Brook had noticed that the dark moon magic in Waywren hovered around the heads of many of the residents, although the dark wisps did not show up continuously. This must indicate that the magic only activated when they thought of certain things or ideas, which from his interactions with Emmy, all seemed to be thoughts related to Morag.

Brook had seen dense congregations of the dark moon magic tendrils leaking from the shaman's hut and the underground place where he knew that Trevi was being held until his trial. That made Brook worried for his friend as he started biting the tips of his fingernails, a bad habit on Alir where ingesting too much stardust was poisonous. The only reason he hadn't attempted a jailbreak was Emmy's insistence that her father would not back down on his word that he would bring Trevi out for the upcoming trial. It would be easier to free him when they brought him out for his trial if they did not just free him as an order of the trial itself. Her head had been clear of the mind fog wisps when she said those words, so Brook believed her, even though it made him uneasy.

Most of their conversations in the forest clearing had been about their findings in the library, or rather, lack of findings. Emmy had been eagerly pointing Brook toward books that she had read growing up. Brook read page after page, but Emmy had already done a spectacular job of relaying all the information in her head to Brook about the starflower and all the ancient languages of Alir that she recognized, that there seemed to be nothing new to find. After Brook whined about it, Emmy suggested that he wander around on his own for a while to seek out anything that she may have missed. There didn't seem to be anything that she had left out when he had completed that search. They had looked for information to exorcise Trevi's demon, but even that was a fruitless endeavor.

Most of the books on demons were on how best to kill or avoid them. All of the exorcising rituals mentioned were standard ones that Trevi had already tried without success.

In an effort to boost Brook's hope, Emmy mentioned that the library had a book checkout system so that patrons could take books home with them, leading to some of them having gone missing over the years. She figured there might be a record of them somewhere, but she hadn't seen one. Morag was a caretaker of the library and took particular interest in any new books that came there. A point that bothered Brook when coupled with his growing suspicions of Morag and dark moon magic. Emmy suggested that he may have records of which books had gone missing. That thought had triggered the mind fog wisps and had caused her to break her train of thought before wandering over to the butterfly tree. Before then, she had been sitting next to Brook on the log, and he could still smell her lovely floral scent when he breathed deeply.

In Emmy's defense, she had been doing pretty well at deterring the mind fog wisps with her light moon magic, but sometimes they snuck in quickly. Part of the reason for them coming out here was that her ability to escape their effects increased the further away from Waywren she was. They couldn't leave until Trevi's trial though, which should be happening this evening. Another part of their reasoning to come out into the woods was to keep their conversations private about their knowledge of the dark moon magic while they gathered more information, and maybe another small part was that they enjoyed spending the time alone together.

Tearing away the peace, Nim came flying unannounced into the forest clearing with great speed and general alarm. Her small wings beat so fast before she stopped to hover that they looked as invisible as those on a hummingbird, "Chaos in Waywren! Trevi has escaped! He was in his demon form, and the villagers are terrified." Nim shuddered midair for effect, making her wide eyes bigger and tucking her clawed paws close to her chest in an attempt to mimic the villager's fear. "The village elder is trying to calm and unite them with Morag standing beside him." The beautiful butterflies disappeared with the appearance of the dragon, taking the peaceful moments with them.

"Oh no," Brook said aloud. "So much for them releasing Trevi after the trial. I wonder, what could have triggered his demonic episode?" Brook thought of the dark moon magic swirls that he had seen escape the prison area. He couldn't begin to fathom what triggered Trevi, but he knew it could not have been good.

"It must have been Morag," Emmy said with the black and white moon wisps warring above her head. Thinking fast, as she always did, she jogged purposely over to Brook and grabbed his hands in hers while looking into his eyes with sincerity and urgency, "You need to hide. They will be looking for you now that your friend has escaped thinking that he may have returned to you. With any luck, maybe we can find Trevi before they do. If the green witches find him in their frightened state, I dare not say what could happen to him. I'll go back to town and see what good I can do to calm my father and the rest of the town. This way they will not be able to claim I have been kidnapped either."

Emmy let go of Brook's hands and eye contact to rummage through her shoulder pack and pulled out a piece of paper with some rough scrawling on it. "Go here." She pointed to a place marked with an 'X' on the map. "This is a secret place where I used to meet my mother, Auraline, before she left Waywren for good. As far as I know, no one else knows of its existence. You should be safe there until I can make it to you. I will come find you as soon as the town is settled, or until they decide to remain unsettled and there is nothing else that I can do about it." She shoved the paper into Brook's pack when he didn't move fast enough for her liking.

"What if they keep you prisoner?" Brook argued back.

"They won't. I am the village elder's daughter and the 'demon' was on trial for attacking me. I can be more help there for our cause than I am here. I promise I will come to find you. Explore the ruins when you get to the secret spot. There is a library there. Maybe, you will find more of what you seek." She cocked her head in consideration before continuing, "Wait for five days. If I don't come back for you, then go search for Trevi. He will need you more than I will."

"But..." Brook started to protest again, but Emmy put her finger to his lips.

"We have to hurry. Thank you, for these past few days of companionship. We will find each other, again, sooner than later. It's shown in the cards." Emmy said before pulling him in for a hug, a real hug meant for him, not one meant to hide their intentions, as the one a few days before had been. That made a difference in Brook's mind, and he could feel the pure warmth of the hug radiant through him as he hugged her back.

With one last shared glance, Emmy pulled away, turned her back towards Brook, and took off at a light jog. Nim flew ahead of her on their way back to Waywren. Brook pulled his new, crinkled map out to examine it. Emmy had made the directions for him from this very spot in the woods, so it shouldn't be too hard to follow. The cards must have told her that she would need it, or else she was a very prepared individual.

***

After a bit of a trek through the woods, Brook had taken out his sword to use it as a machete through the dense plant growth. With each slice, occasional puffs of star shavings would escape causing him to cover his eyes to prevent the sting of its impact. There were the remnants of a very old path beneath the foliage that he was hacking back, indicating that maybe this secret location wasn't so secret a great many years ago.

Brook saw trickles of sunlight widen through the trees up ahead and thought that there might be a clearing. If that wasn't the location of the hiding place, he may take a moment to sit and write about his day. He was exhausted, and a good writing session always seemed to do wonders on his nerves.

He was worried about Trevi, he was worried about Emmy, and he was having feelings about Emmy that he'd swore he'd never have, but wouldn't acknowledge them fully. Yet, he was still excited about all the progress that had been made on the mystery of the ring. Brook felt guilty about that excitement since he was the only one of his friends that was safe. He needed time to gather his thoughts and sort through his emotions before doing anything else. He was getting overwhelmed and tired, both in the physical and emotional sense.

Brook stepped cautiously into the clearing, eyeing the bushes and trees as though an enemy might ambush him from behind any one of them. Once he felt sufficiently safe, he found a tree to lean his back against and rest, tipping his head to the skies and breathing out slowly before taking in the view in front of him. In the center of the clearing, there were the ruins of a structure sticking up from the ground like jagged wooden teeth in the maw of an aging predator. Some pieces were sharp, some were dull, some were missing, and all were rotten. They were so old and rotted, that it was impossible to tell what that structure might have been.

Brook concluded that this must be the location marked by the prominent 'X' on Emmy's map. Instead of pulling out his writing paraphernalia, he stepped forward toward the ruins, letting his curiosity win out. There should be a hatch in the ground that he could pull up according to the notes that Emmy had left. Brook started sweeping his foot across the ground, wiping the dirt and stardust clumps away. He found a handle. Emmy said that it wouldn't be locked, so he grabbed it with two hands and gave it a good yank upward. It opened easily, and Brook found himself on his rump in a cloud of dirt and star shavings. He stood up, brushed himself off, and then took a peek into the cellar that descended from the hatch. Stone stairs were carved into it.

He took the stairs slowly into the darkness, where the only light that was let in was from the open hatch. After some fumbling around in the dark, Brook found a lantern and lit it up. The cellar must have been someone's study at some point because there were walls lined with bookshelves and a desk with an ink pot and stacks of paper on it against one of the walls. Brook approached the desk with the lantern in his hand and saw a leather-bound book. He brushed the cover off with his free hand and found words etched into the leather cover. He angled the lantern slightly closer so he could read them: JOURNAL OF JAX PELLON.

Pellon…it took a moment to hit Brook. He was a Pellon. Could this be the journal of one of his ancestors? Could this be the journal of his *originally* cursed ancestor? He almost dropped the lantern in shock as he stumbled backward a few steps with his heart pounding loudly in his chest. After recovering, he lifted the lantern more firmly with his hand to look at the books on the shelves. He had to wipe them down to read the titles written on their exposed spines: The Art of Blacksmithing, Gemstone Facet Design, How to Cut Gemstones, Starfire vs. Moonlight, Botany for Beginners, Advanced Botany of Magical Plants, The Crystal Alchemist, Crystal Grids: How and Why They Work, Properties of Light: Star, Moon, and Sun, Old Languages and Linguistics, and so many more. Had he missed something throughout the years? Why did this Pellon have so many books on crystals and gemstones?

Brook slid the ring off of his finger and examined

the emerald gemstone more closely. It was cut in a very unique and extravagant manner; unlike any other gemstone he had seen in the past. Not that Brook had seen many gemstones, admittedly. His family hadn't lived a wealthy lifestyle. He also couldn't see very well in the dim lantern light to judge. He would have to study these books and look through the journal to see if they had any answers.

Brook felt so close now. The answers were in this room; they had to be! Hidden away in the dusty old books and papers like gold pieces within a treasure chest. His exhaustion melted away and was replaced by an eagerness to jump into all of the books here and swim around in the treasures within. He would start with Jax's journal. That would hopefully give him an idea of what books to search through next based on whatever Jax had written.

Brook tripped slightly on his way back over to the desk. There must have previously been a wooden chair because rotten wood scraps littered the floor in front of the desk. If he looked close enough, he could see that tiny bugs were crawling around in it. Gross. He hoped that age and vermin hadn't desecrated any of the information in this treasure trove. He kicked the wooden remains into an isolated pile and leaned over the desk to admire the journal, his first treasure chest to open.

He carefully tried to lift the cover of the journal, and he could feel the delicacy of the ancient materials. Brook may not have had magic or a dragon familiar, but he did know a lot about paper and writing. With any luck, Jax would have used similar chemicals that Brook did to make his paper more formidable to the passing of time. Brook had wanted to ensure that his messages in bottles were preserved for years past him, so he had taken to learning about the intricacies of paper. He had a bottle of the solution that he coated all his paper within his pack. If Brook could get the pages of Jax's journal to survive the first opening of the book, then he could paint them with that solution and be more confident in their survival as he studied.

***

The birds chirped their morning song in welcome of the new day as Trevi cooked his breakfast over the small fire that he had made. There hadn't been a starstorm in a few days so hunting was easier. There were no piles of stardust against trees, muddied-up ponds, or sparkle-freckled plants that creatures could hide in. That was the one good thing that Trevi had going for him. He sighed, looking down at his black and red carapace arm rotating the makeshift spit over the fire as he licked his fanged teeth in anticipation of a meal.

It had been days since he escaped from his confines in Waywren, and he still had not transformed back to his human form. That vial of poison that Morag injected him with must have forced his demonic transformation in such a way that it was either permanent or harder to reverse. Trevi knew that he had reached his ultimate calmness, and even then, this form remained. All his anger had passed at the situation, and he was attempting to figure out how to live like this. Brook wasn't a problem. He would just have to explain what happened to him. But how would he go about in public places? He could try living here, in the wilds of the Silvertree forest. Trevi had grown adept at hunting and scavenging. He could just build himself a secluded hut, like Emmy, but what if an outsider located him? They would no doubt want to kill a demon on sight.

Trevi shook his head. These were important matters, yes, but there was something more pressing at the moment. He had information on Brook's father to get to him, and information on Morag's treachery to get to Emmy. Unfortunately, he had no idea where they were. If they were still in Waywren, he couldn't go back there. Morag would surely be waiting for him. Trevi was not only a prime candidate for his soul collection, but he had also seen something that Morag had been keeping secret from the rest of the people of Waywren. If Trevi's conversations with Emmy had any basis in truth, then the green witches would condemn Morag for using dark moon magic. There was no way that Morag would let Trevi live after seeing that secret of his.

Trevi wondered if Morag knew what his poison would do to Trevi. He must have known that it would transform him into a demon, but did he know that he would keep his human mind? Did he know that Trevi would be able to comprehend things beyond pure rage as he traversed his secret laboratory? Trevi wasn't sure if he would ever find that out, but he guessed that with Morag's cunning, he probably had known that Trevi would make an escape after being turned into a demon. He had practically invited it by the way he had walked out the dungeon's door immediately after the transformation.

Of course, he would have wanted Trevi to escape at midday. That was when many of the residents of Waywren were active for the day and would be most likely to see Trevi emerge as a demon. If Trevi frightened the villagers themselves, then he would most assuredly lose his trial, and Morag would be able to harvest Trevi's demon soul without people caring where Trevi disappeared to in the aftermath. That left a pretty big unanswered question for Trevi. What was Morag's scheme to retrieve his prized demon soul after the planned midday prison break?

Trevi stamped out the fire with his fire-resistant feet, then ate his breakfast as he chased the smoke away with large leaf fronds. He would need to move more stealthily from now on. He was no doubt being hunted, or soon to be.

CHAPTER 10: AUSPICIOUS AURALINE

*T*revi refused to the let angry side of the demon control him. His body may be that of a horrid creature, but that didn't mean he had to let his mind and attitude succumb. At times, his body quivered at the strength of the defense that he put up against the demonic rage demanding to be let out, but Trevi was mentally strong. He had been inadvertently training for this for years. He was the epitome of control and calm when he wanted to be. He wouldn't let Morag's detestable mob chasing him push him over the edge, no matter how irrational and abusive they were with their knives and pitchforks raised.

He had made it partway to the Alveni mountains, but the persistent crowd still followed him. He wasn't sure if they were wholly consistent of the green witches from Waywren, but a portion of them must have been encouraged by Morag. Trevi had not been willing to let them get close enough to find out for sure.

Hatred filled the voices of the people in the woods as they chanted "Kill the demon! Kill the demon!" Over and over again. It was almost inhuman the way they pursued him. One hive mind turned to one purpose. Somehow, they had even been able to keep up with his fast demon dashing. He supposed if they were green witches, they probably had some sort of magical means to aid them. Maybe a dragon familiar was tracking him.

Trevi was currently hidden in a cave that he had found dug out near the base of two large trees. He clung to the darkened ceiling, tucked into an overhang. His demon claws dug into the rock of the cave enabling him not to slip down. He hoped his pursuers would either pass the cave or if they entered, that they would walk straight under him and not notice that he was there, then he could double back behind them. That was a new tactic that he hadn't tried yet. He was getting tired of this chase and a little nagging voice at the edge of his mind played with the idea of turning himself in so he could finally get some rest. He had to keep his mind strong against that idea infiltrating too far, as well.

"Trevi," a soft voice spoke with slight echoes deeper within the ceiling cave crevice that he clung to. Oh great, Trevi thought, now he was going crazy.

"Trevi, this way, I'll show you a way out," the voice came again. This time Trevi dipped his chin between his chest and the ceiling to see that the crevice he was in did indeed go further if he were to wedge himself in just a bit more. A faint, inviting glow illuminated the area within. Thinking he'd run out of choices, he decided to trust the sweet-sounding voice over his luck with the rampaging villagers.

Trevi inched and squeezed himself into the hole. At first, it smushed his chest so tightly that he never thought that he would make it through. Then with one last heave, he burst out the other side of the hole, tail first. He landed on his feet since he was in demon form, and with that came all the reflexes and grace of the beast's body.

A small globe of white light glowed in the dark cave, floating in the air, awaiting his arrival. It looked a little like Sammy, the eavesdropping sentrifly that Emmy had summoned to listen in on Trevi and Brook's conversations at her house, but it was slightly different in its coloration and in the way the swirls moved. "Follow me," it said in the same soft and soothing voice, bobbing up and down while levitating only a few feet from Trevi. The presence of the sentrifly was familiar to Trevi, and it seemed less dangerous than the mob that had been chasing him for hours now, so he decided to trust it further. It wasn't afraid of Trevi's demon form, which was a first from any creature or human that he had met, so it deserved a chance.

Trevi nodded his head and the light started weaving its way through the cave tunnels which it brightened just by being there. Eventually, Trevi could not hear the raging mob behind him, and he could see an even larger light at the end of the tunnel that he was being led towards. At some point in his life, he was sure someone had told him "Don't go towards the light," but this one seemed to emanate goodness, and he had gone too far to turn around. All there was behind him was an angry mob screaming for his blood. There was no way he could thwart them forever and also find Brook or Emmy.

He turned the last corner of darkness and found himself looking in awe at a bright, yellow light dragon as it stared down at him with neon green eyes from a sitting posture in the back of the cave dwelling. It wasn't quite as large as the black dragon that he had met earlier, but it was much larger than Emmy's green dragon Nim. Its tail coiled around its body showing off the electric green spines that lined its body from head to tail. Little sparks of electricity jumped from spine to spine on occasion creating a crackling noise and a spark of light. The scales overlapping one another along the skin of the dragon shifted from yellow to golden in the changing light patterns of the cave's room. On top of its long neck, its elongated nose hid the sharp teeth within its muzzle, unlike Trevi's muzzle which let the tips of his sharp demonic teeth poke through to increase his intimidation factor. Except for the electricity jumps across its spines to keep you on edge, this light dragon looked like a pretty chill creature.

The eyes of the creature inspected him closely but showed no outward fear or aggression towards Trevi's demonic form. Trevi realized that he had been holding himself stiff in apprehension since rounding the corner and allowed his muscles to ease into a more relaxed posture.

"Welcome, Trevi," the familiar soft voice came from the side of the side of the cavern nearest the dragon's head. Trevi turned to see a middle-aged lady with long, dark brown hair held back with a jeweled headband. One of her hands was on the dragon's body as if to soothe the creature. Her dress looked as though she had made it mimic the yellow and gold of the light dragon's scales which allowed for her rich brown hair to stand out. "I am Auraline. This is my familiar, Lumeni. Emmy has told you a little about me?"

"Auraline," Trevi whispered to himself, and then his eyes brightened as he remembered. "Yes. She has. You are Emmy's mother. The one who left Waywren."

"Yes, that is me. Emmy and I have remained in touch through other means since then, even though we haven't seen each other physically. Our ties to moon magic enable these interactions. I had to leave Waywren since Morag held Renier, my husband's, ear closer than I did. Even though I could see through Morag's schemes, I couldn't convince Renier that his mentor since childhood was betraying him and using him against the very town that he swore to protect."

"Morag was using dark moon magic, but Renier would not listen to me and scolded me each time I broached the subject. Morag was doing his best to get rid of me and turn Renier and the town against me since I knew his secret. I wouldn't let him mind control me like he did the rest of the village since I was able to put up defenses around my mind knowing there was a danger. Well, it was more of mind *suggesting* than outright tampering. He didn't mess with old memories or create false ones, he only nudged certain thoughts away when they came up. Regardless, I was not strong enough to take him down myself, or to protect the others in the village from his mind games, so I went into hiding to one day find some help to take him down and free Waywren of his taint."

Trevi shook his demonic head, "Well, I don't think I'll be of much help to you. Look at me. I'm a worthless demon who everyone wants dead."

Auraline spoke with an encouraging note to her voice, "A demon who must know something Morag doesn't want him to know since he sent that mob after you. A demon with a human heart. As a matter of fact, I'd say you aren't a demon at all, just a boy trapped within the skin of a demon."

It was true Trevi thought. He was a prisoner in his own body. Auraline could see it. She was treating him as the human he was. That brought more hope to Trevi. Auraline was a special woman.

"You're right. I do know something that Morag doesn't want me to know. I know that he is using dark moon magic to maintain an eternal life for himself at the cost of my friend, Brook's, family line, and maybe others. He steals their life away after they hit forty years old and stores their souls within his secret laboratory where his soul sucks the energy out of the living souls. I saw it with my own eyes since I can see dark moon magic in this demonic body prison. I saw the dark tendrils of mist connecting his victims' souls to his own."

"He also forced my body into this form using some sort of poison that he injected into me. It was probably something that he made from a spell book that I saw in his laboratory. He said something about adding demonic blood to his soul collection. So, I am guessing that he wants to add my soul to his soul collection in hopes that my demonic blood will somehow make him stronger. I'm betting he forced me into a demon to help guarantee that type of soul."

It was Auraline's turn to shake her head, "Even if he were to succeed with his hopes to add you to his soul collection, he would have been sorely disappointed. You are a human in your soul, not a demon. A demon would not be conversing with me, but instead be driven by pure rage. As with the moon, you are whole no matter what phase you are in." A thoughtful look crossed her face before changing the subject away from Trevi, "I hadn't realized that he was using dark moon magic to extend his life. I wonder if I was as immune to his mind tricks as I thought that I was to have missed something so big. He has been alive for generations. That is not normal."

Auraline started pacing as she thought out loud, "Dark moon magic is forbidden not because it comes from the dark side of the moon, but because the means by which it creates its ends are never kind. Eternal life in itself isn't wrong, but obtaining it by stealing the lives of others is. The general green witch population strives to be kind to all living creatures, but there are always a few transgressors who believe that a little of another's pain is worth their success and power. That is why we have forbidden it in our order. It is not right what Morag has done to your friend's family. If the souls still exist in his laboratory, there should be a way to free them, but we would have to get through Morag first and then break the curse from there."

Trevi piped up in an attempt to be helpful, "Brook, my friend has a ring. It is passed down from generation to generation with the supposition that it contains the answer to breaking the curse on his family. He has been trying to decipher it his whole life."

Auraline nodded, "Emmy mentioned this in our last meeting. She also mentioned that Brook is waiting for me at our old hideout in the woods. I can bring you to him."

Trevi perked up in excitement, "Yes, I would appreciate that! I need to talk to him soon."

Auraline started to pet the light dragon, almost

seeming to need it to calm herself. "There is one more thing that I need to tell you. Emmy is in danger. She went back to Waywren after you had escaped. She had thought to save you the accusations of kidnapping her and hoped to calm the town down, but she was unsuccessful. Renier now holds her hostage within Waywren, not allowing her to leave even though she is in the comfortable confines of his house and not within Morag's dungeons. She needs to be rescued before Morag can completely wipe her mind. I had encouraged her to leave Waywren years ago and had hoped she'd be safe. I don't know how long she can keep defenses up in town with Morag directly working on her."

"We need to save her then!" Trevi said with vehemence. He wouldn't let one of his few friends be taken away so easily.

"I thought you would say as much," Auraline said with a smile. "The only way that I know of to defeat Morag's dark moon magic-protected self is with condensed starlight: starfire. Starfire will not break the curses he has created, but it should sever through his defenses and finally send Morag to his final resting place where he should have been so long ago. I can call on little bits of this at night with the help of my moon magic, but getting a concentrated amount of it contained for long enough to use against Morag has proven tricky. I would love to get a look at your friend's ring when we get to him. I truly do hope that it does have the answers."

***

Brook was mentally salivating at all the information in the treasure trove that Emmy had given him the map to. He had never been so engrossed in his reading and research. He looked almost as though he was becoming one of the books that he was reading with the dirt and stardust clinging to his hair and exposed skin.

The text carved into the ring said "Harnesser of Light." That was the name Jax had given it. The ring's emerald gemstone was faceted to hold starlight inside of it. Jax had done the handiwork himself. There was a piece of a starflower within the ring that he had hoped when powered by the starlight would grant wishes, but it hadn't worked. When Brook examined the ring closely in the light of the lantern, he could see the paper-like piece of flower within the gem.

Incredible. Jax must have found a real starflower before crafting the ring. Proof that starflowers did exist! Brook hoped that somewhere among Jax's notes that he had made a map of its location. Maybe, if he could put the starflower back together, it would grant him the wish to free his family from the forty-year curse! Brook had forgotten what real hope had felt like until now. That hope is what drove his intense study fervor.

One thing bothered him. Emmy had memorized all the material in the library in Waywren to tell him about starflowers and ancient Alirian writing. Why hadn't she told him about the information here? Why would she keep this a secret from him? She should have memorized this material just as well as the material in Waywren if she had read it.

Brook must have mumbled his misgivings out loud

because they were answered by an unfamiliar soft, sweet voice, "It's because she hadn't read any of these books. I didn't let her touch anything when we met here because I didn't want there to be any easy trails to trace back to her. I wanted the place to look as untouched as possible."

Brook turned around slowly, leaving his current book open to the page he was on. The only person Emmy had said that she had ever met here was her mother, Auraline. He saw her when he turned around.

"Auraline?" He asked, just to be sure.

"Yes, it is me," she said, then the tone of her voice changed to reflect a slight tone of reprisal. "She was correct in her description of you. So quick to judge, even your friends. Emmy did not hide anything from you, yet you were so sure that she had."

"I'm sorry, Auraline," Brook said guiltily. What a way to make a first impression on a girl's mother. "She reprimanded me for doing the same with my friend Trevi whom I've known since childhood. I am trying to get better."

"Don't fret too much on it now," Auraline said, "We have other, more pressing, problems to resolve." She looked up the hatch that they had entered through and called, "We're ready for you!"

Auraline backed away from the hatch and a demon climbed down into the cellar, barely fitting his bulk through the hatched doorway. Was that Trevi? He was never calm as a demon. Brook's hand moved cautiously over to his sword hilt before he met the eyes of the demon. They were blue with only a hint of red, not the deep red of the true demon that Trevi would transform into. He let go of his sword hilt.

"Trevi? What happened?" Brook looked his friend over and felt pity for him. He knew how much he hated his demon form.

"Morag injected me with poison. I don't know how to change back. I've tried. No matter how calm I am, the demon shell remains," Trevi responded with a shrug of his huge, black and red, mottled arms. It would have been a comical move for a horrifying creature to make if the situation hadn't been so bad.

"I'm so sorry," was all Brook could say. No words seem good enough.

"Don't worry, my friend. We will fix this. Auraline and Emmy will help us," Trevi said with a smile. That smile though, phew. If Brook hadn't known Trevi to be who he was, he would have run in terror at those exposed piercing teeth.

The next few hours they caught each other up on what had happened. Trevi told Brook what had happened in Morag's labs, Auraline told them of her moon magic correspondences with Emmy and her current predicament in Waywren, and Brook told them of what he had found in this secret cellar.

When they were done, Auraline asked Brook to see his ring. He held it out for her to look at, but she gave him a look that said, "Hand it over." He relinquished it with apprehension into her open hand. Auraline inspected the gemstone and froze when she caught sight of the piece of petal from the starflower. She stared at it before saying anything.

"I have an idea of how to fix our situation, but I think we need to divide and conquer. Not only ourselves but this ring." She said with determination before turning to Brook. "How would you feel about removing the piece of starflower from this ring and giving it to Trevi to traverse the mountains in search of the starflower while you and I imbue this ring with starfire and go to Waywren to vanquish Morag and rescue Emmy?"

Brook replied honestly, "Hesitant. The ring and my family have been together for so long, but none of us knew of the flower within."

Auraline responded, "Even Jax admits in his notes that the ring did not work as designed. My thought is if we can make the flower whole again, then its wishing power will be restored."

"How will we know where to find the flower?" Brook asked, still hesitant to do anything to despoil the ring.

"This map," Auraline said as she moved a few books to the side, waving away the dusty residue that their movement made in the air with a slight cough, and delicately pulled out a very old piece of loose paper folded over on itself.

"I thought you said you hadn't read any of the material down here," Brook said defensively noting how easily she found the map and the fact that she knew that the ring was broken from Jax's original intention. Brook had only learned the latter by reading Jax's journal.

"I said Emmy had not read the books down here, not that I hadn't," Auraline said dismissively. "You are deflecting though. I was hoping we could all agree upon the possible solution track before taking it. It is your ring after all. It wouldn't be right to alter it without your permission. My light moon magic will be able to extract the piece of petal without harm to the rest of the ring or the petal. If you didn't know it wasn't there, you wouldn't notice. So, it would just be like it was to you before you found this cellar."

Brook considered. It did seem like their only plan that covered all bases quickly. If her moon magic could remove the petal, she could likely get it back inside later, if needed. "Okay, fine," Brook complied begrudgingly. "Remove the petal and give it to Trevi with the map. If any of us can survive the wilderness, it is him."

"Atta boy," Auraline said with a ring of approval in her voice, and before Brook could change his mind, his ring was floating above Auraline's hand. He couldn't see the moon magic because he wasn't wearing the ring, but it looked magical enough as the sliver of a petal removed itself from the small slit in the gemstone of the ring and both objects landed softly back into Auraline's hand.

Brook had a thought, but it was too late to go back now, "Will I still be able to see moon magic with the petal gone?"

Auraline handed him back the ring which he greedily grabbed for when it was offered, "I can't say for sure, but I would think yes, you will. My theory is that it was the encapsulated starlight that allowed you to see moon magic. Nothing to do with the petal of the starflower. Starfire is condensed starlight. It is the only known entity that can vanquish moon magic, it makes sense that it could be connected to that. Your ancestor also sealed this ring in his blood, your blood. Making its connection to only people descended from him. This explains why it only allowed you to see moon magic. I assume it would have let your father see it, as well.

How about you give it a try since I don't know for sure? Your ancestor created a very unique artifact."

Brook swiftly slipped the ring back onto his finger and looked eagerly at Auraline. She smiled and used moon magic to summon her divination deck from her belongings.

"I saw it! I saw it!" Brook said excitedly as he watched the silvery blue wisps play around the hovering card deck before they placed it back into Auraline's pack.

"Good," Auraline said and then turned her attention to Trevi. She placed the delicate starflower petal into the palm of his savage demonic hand. It looked so pretty, tiny, and out of place, but he cradled it with high respect. "You'll have to take good care of this on your journey." Trevi nodded as he put it in a small wrapping within a pouch that he had crafted during his days in the wilderness after being expelled from Waywren. "You'll need this, too." She handed him the map. He had a bit of trouble unfolding it with his claws, but he was getting used to them. Eventually, he got it open and stared at the map intensely before refolding it and putting it away. Brook assumed he must have memorized as much as he could have before he tucked it into his pouch. It would be difficult for him with his claws to have to reference the physical map frequently.

"Brook, come with me for a minute," Auraline insisted after Trevi had his petal and map stored safely away. She climbed up the cellar stairs. Brook didn't know how many days he had been here, nor if it were night or day. He should have been counting since Emmy had told him a certain number of days before leaving, but he had just gotten so lost in his research that he forgot to keep track. When you do the same thing each day, it's difficult to distinguish the passing of time. No need to chide himself now. He stepped up to the cellar door, looked up the steps, and noted the hue of the sky before following Auraline up into the night.

Stars bloomed across the sky with the moon in a partial phase creating a bright pistil for them to congregate around. "They are beautiful," Brook said, almost to himself.

Auraline chuckled, "Yes, they are. Not many people stay out late enough under clear enough skies to see this artistic masterpiece. There are powers greater than magic at work on these nights that not many people realize. Did you know that some people think that the stars have prescience of their own?"

"I hadn't," Brook replied. "But it makes sense. There are many different religions."

Auraline nodded, "When you truly open yourself to the night skies and feel the energy flowing in, it's hard to think otherwise. Why don't you give it a try and see what happens?"

"Me? I have no magic, I don't know how to feel energy," Brook shook his head dejectedly.

Auraline encouraged him, "Oh, but I think you do. You've seen moon magic with your ring. Try to find a sense of inner peace and listen with your heart. You may be surprised at what you find."

Brook took a deep breath and closed his eyes, letting the stars watch him instead of he looking at them. What did he have to lose from trying? Nothing. For a minute, nothing happened, but then he imagined the starlight flowing into him and flowing into the ring. He felt warm, tingly, and energized. Could it have worked? He let the feeling propagate through his entire body for a while before he finally let go and reopened his eyes.

"Did it work?" was all he had to say upon his return from the stars.

Auraline smiled at him, "Take a look at your ring and tell me what you think."

Brook looked down at the emerald ring and saw the gem sporting a dim glow. "I did that?" he asked with astonishment while pointing at it with his other hand.

"Yes," Auraline said sincerely, "You did that."

"Is it enough?" Brook wondered.

Auraline seemed to know what he meant because she answered his question, "It has to be because we need to defeat Morag to save Emmy and free Waywren." Brook frowned at her, not liking the lack of certainty in her response. She continued, "I've not had a contraption to condense starlight into starfire and contain it. This is new to me, too. I only know the theory behind it all. If you can direct the power of the starfire within the ring towards Morag when we get to Waywren, then you should be able to defeat him since the starfire can penetrate dark moon magic. Your intuition will have to guide you from there, just as it did tonight when you filled the ring with the light of the stars."

Brook sighed and felt the heavy weight of responsibility on his shoulders. He saw Trevi's demonic form clamber out of the cellar to join them under the night sky. A shade of doubt cast over Brook at the sight of Trevi in demon form. How could he trust his friend to make the right wish on the starflower, to free his family from the curse, if he wasn't there? Brook caught himself this time. First, he should trust his friend. Second, how did Brook know that freeing his family from the forty-year curse was more important than exorcising Trevi's demonic form?

Brook let his eyes linger on Trevi and realized just how strong he was. Not just Trevi's body, but his soul. How many people could live completely encapsulated in evil and still bring out the light within themselves? He knew he certainly had trouble being nice to people on the days when everything went wrong, but never did he remember Trevi scolding him for it. And here Trevi was, trapped in his worst nightmare, and he was still his same self, as always.

Brook realized then that he could learn a lot from his friend. He trusted Trevi to make the right choice with the starflower when the time came. Whatever the right choice might be. This journey that they had been on since childhood was just as much Trevi's as it was Brook's. They were both co-stars. He was not a leader and Trevi his devout follower. If anything, it was the other way around. Brook was not going to judge Trevi with whatever decision he made when he reached the starflower.

Suddenly, Brook felt the weight of responsibility lighten on his shoulders. He had acknowledged Trevi as his equal and knew he could truly count on and support his friend in all of his decisions. He didn't need to waste his worry on him. They were the best of friends. They were family.

CHAPTER 11: GARDENER OF THE STARS

The mountain air was cold, but the demon's soul was a fire never extinguished. Trevi wondered if this was how the red dragons felt. Bitter cold winds biting at their noses, but a hot fire burning inside that never let their inner core get frozen. He wondered if he would get to meet a red dragon on his journey to the starflower. He had met green, yellow, black, and white dragons on Alir, so far. To get the full set, he would just need to find a red and blue one. Trevi chuckled to himself which was a strange sound to come from a demon's body. This wasn't a collector card game, but he had to keep himself entertained as he navigated the wilderness alone. In truth, he did not hope to meet a dragon, even in his demon form. The black dragon had already proven how powerless even demon Trevi was against a dragon.

He was getting close to the area marked on Jax's map now. It was nighttime, which was good since he thought that he would have an easier time finding the flower in the darkness with its characteristic glow. Trevi's biggest worry was if it was still there or not. He didn't know how many years, decades, maybe centuries it had been since Jax had last visited this flower. It might have been stumbled across by another creature in all those years. Although, it was in a very secluded, hard to get to, part of the Alveni mountains making it possible that it could have been overlooked. Or maybe the flower had just died from natural weather conditions or a plant disease. No. Trevi could not think that way. This flower was their shining beacon of hope. He would find it.

Trevi ascended the steep, rocky ground with relative ease in his demon body. His claws could gain a grasp where fingers would have failed. His innate balance was working wonders on the narrow paths with a sheer drop on one side into a rocky oblivion that would have given a lesser human vertigo. Pebbles would roll off the ledges, but Trevi was a boulder. Steady and strong. There was one steep incline left which should lead to a cliff overhang that had a clear view of the stars each night. That was where Jax had marked the starflower's location.

With one last heave from his upper arm muscles, his back feet dug into the rock and propelled his body forward onto the top of the cliff. Trevi stood up and looked around. The wind blew cold. Its gusts may have been strong enough to push a small child off the ledge, but Trevi was no small child. It whipped up bits of rocks and rubble which flung towards Trevi's face in protest of him being here, but he was easily able to evade the projectiles with his hands and quick head movements.

At last, he spotted it. Pixie dust, the starflower's pollen, speckled the huge, floppy petals and the ground around the massive flower, like glitter on a ballgown. The flower itself was a blend of sky blues, ceruleans, and teals. It shined brilliantly, like a star that had fallen from the sky onto the cliffside, gazing longingly back up to its home. Trevi approached the ancient flower reverently. The description that Emmy gave of the starflower did not do the sight of it justice.

Once he was within touching distance, Trevi removed the piece of the petal from his pack. He could have sworn that the starflower flickered. Was it reacting to the piece of a petal that Trevi pulled out? Trevi inspected the flower without touching it. It felt right to try and find the original placement of this petal piece. It was a difficult search with all of the overlaying petals, and Trevi thought that he might have to start looking underneath them when he found what he was looking for. One of the bottom petals, at the very top tip, had a small piece carefully torn out of it.

He gingerly held the petal piece in his hand close to the injured plant's petal while sitting in a hunched position on the ground. When the petal piece touched its home on the original petal, the pollen started shifting towards the severed section and wound itself into glittering strands of thread before proceeding to sew it back together. It really did look like pixie dust as it magically wove the broken petal back into its whole condition. Once the last thread was pulled through, the seam tightened itself and a glittering scar remained. The starflower was whole once more.

Trevi backed away as he watched the flower brighten even more. It was magnificent and mesmerizing. He knew that he should make his wish now, but how could he put something this beautiful back together and then chance killing it? He still didn't know how to save the flower after making his wish.

"Hello," a feminine ethereal voice sounded to his side. "What ails you?"

Trevi turned his head away from the starflower to see a silver-haired maiden with skin matching the shades of blue of the starflower petals, sparkling with its own glittering sheen. She wore a flowing, white dress that seemed impervious to the winds as she floated a few feet off the ground next to him with a concerned look on her face.

"Who are you?" Trevi asked, "Aren't you afraid of me?"

"I am the spirit of the star that inhabits this flower. You have braved many dangers and discomforts to make me whole again. Why would I fear you?"

Trevi answered, "I am stuck in this demon form. Everyone fears it. At least, I used to think that. I am starting to find that some are willing to look beyond appearances."

"You are a smart boy. Is that what your wish was going to be? To free yourself from the demon that resides inside of you?" the star spirit asked curiously.

"I...I don't know, to be honest. You see, I have heard that the reason starflowers are scarce is because once a wish is made then the flower itself dies. I just don't know if I can bring myself to do that. But if I don't, then my friend Brook and his family will continue to lose their minds at the age of forty to feed a shaman's desire for eternal life." Trevi responded in a voice that resonated with his inner conflict.

The star spirit studied him before responding, "What if I told you that there was a way to save and regrow starflowers?"

Trevi looked up at her with eager eyes, "Tell me, please! I'll do it! I don't want to have to hurt something to save something else."

"Ah, yes," the star spirit said, "You have the heart of a true green witch. That is one of their core values." The spirit snapped her fingers and a book made of a transparent, blueish flame appeared out of thin air before landing in her palms. She handed it to Trevi who noticed that it did not have any substantial material to it. His hand could pass through it, or if he had the mind to grab the book, it was solid enough for him to hold.

"It's made of starfire," she explained before encouraging him, "Take a look through it. This starfire is safe to touch."

Trevi turned to the first page and started reading it to himself before he realized that he was reading a language that he had never learned. Wasn't this the language that was inscribed upon the side of Brook's ring? He had seen that many times before, but never had been able to read it.

"How can I read this?" Trevi asked.

"The same way you can see me," the star spirit replied. "Your demonic form can see *all* types of magic. We stars have never been able to interact with anyone who has made wishes with us before because they could not perceive us with their senses. You are special. The same thing which you hate about yourself is the thing that gives you so many unique abilities."

"So, if I become fully human, then I won't be able to see or read this book to save the starflowers?" Trevi said, coming to a stark realization.

"Anything is possible with a wish," the star spirit

replied with a flourish of her hand.

Trevi stood in contemplation for a while. His decision had become more complicated. He could wish for Brook's bloodline to be released from the forty-year curse and keep the ability to read this book to save and repopulate the starflowers at the cost of remaining a demon the rest of his life and hiding from society. Or, he could wish to become fully human, but keep the ability to see all magic. If he did the latter, he could repopulate the starflowers, but Brook would never forgive him for forsaking him and his family. Maybe he could grow another starflower and make whichever wish he didn't make now when it matured?

"How long does it take to grow a starflower to the point where it could grant a wish?" Trevi inquired.

"The flower itself is not what grants wishes, but the star spirit that dwells within. If you garden well enough, your starflowers will attract the spirits of stars to reside inside of them. This will grant the hosting flower eternal life until a wish is made. When a wish has been made, the star spirit is forced to return to the stars since their power is significantly reduced, and they cannot hold themselves away from the skies anymore. The time this takes can be anywhere from ten years to an eternity. It depends on how desirable that you make the flower to a star spirit."

"Ten years, or never," Trevi whispered under his breath. He shook his head. He knew what wish he would have to make. He looked back up to the star spirit, "And you are willing to return to the stars when I make a wish?"

She looked at him with her unreadable, silvery blue eyes, "Yes. I have been here for generations. I have faith that you will succeed in your gardening, and I will be able to inhabit another starflower in this world again."

"What about the flower itself?" Trevi asked looking at the brilliant beauty in front of him.

"She has lived a life longer than any flower can without being inhabited by a star spirit. She will go back into the soil, provide nurture to other living things, and then emerge again as something even greater than what she was. There is no need to mourn either of us. We will both return to this world." Trevi nodded at her words. "What is more important is this: Do you think you are capable of doing what is written in the book to care for starflowers?"

Trevi spent the next few minutes skimming the content of the starflower gardening book. It was quite demanding and time-consuming. He would have to devote his life to this practice. He found a section about preserving a starflower after a wish. He pointed to it and started to read it aloud to the star spirit.

"No!" she slammed the books shut, catching Trevi by surprise.

"What's wrong?" Trevi asked. I was just going to ask you why I shouldn't just do that portion of the book to maintain your presence here in the starflower after I make a wish.

"You must never read a word of this book aloud. This knowledge must be kept secret. The ability to grant any wish is too powerful to be accidentally stolen. Hence the nature of the ethereal book that only you can read."

"Oh. I'm sorry. I didn't realize that. I will be more careful in the future." Trevi eagerly flipped back open to that page, "So, you have no qualms if I try to save you and the starflower after my wish using that section of the book instead of waiting for your return?"

"That is a very difficult procedure to pull off, I wouldn't want you to feel bad if you failed. Even if you were successful, I would not be strong enough to grant another wish again for many years," the star spirit warned.

"Do you want to remain on Alir in this flower?" Trevi asked her.

The star spirit looked to the sky, to the starflower, and finally back to Trevi. "I actually would, if possible. I have nurtured her since she was a seedling."

"Then consider it done. I will not fail you," Trevi promised her.

The star spirit beamed back at him, not only with a smile but with flashes of brilliant cyan light. "You are one of a kind. What is your name, future gardener?"

"Trevi."

"Very well, I name you: Trevi, Gardener of the Stars," the star spirit spoke with conviction and Trevi felt something within him grow.

"What happened?" Trevi asked.

"I have connected your soul with the starflower gardening book. When you unhand it, it will shelve itself in your heart until you call upon it again. This will keep the book protected from anyone else seeing it. The information is internalized within you."

"Clever," Trevi responded.

The star spirit smiled in response. "Well, Trevi, how about that wish you were going to make?"

Trevi looked at the ethereal spirit, hovering there awaiting his words. She was beautiful in a timeless sense. He couldn't tell her age. She was humanoid in a fashion, but almost too slender, like a child in adult form. Her ears peeked into sharp points just above the top of her head through her long, straight, silver hair. Her eyes were the depths of space with silvery blue swirls in the center surrounding a dark pupil.

"Is there anything else that you'd like to say before I make the wish?" Trevi asked the creature before him that was just as magnificent as the starflower behind him.

"Good luck, Trevi. I've put all my faith in you, and I know you'll do well."

Trevi smiled at the star spirit and as delicately as he could with his clawed hand, he lifted a petal of the starflower as if to hold its hand. The star spirit took his other hand in hers. He cleared his heart of all additional thought and concentrated on the one thing that he knew that he desired most.

Trevi spoke with confidence and clarity, "I wish for the curse to be broken on any bloodlines that Morag has tainted to gain his eternal life." He worded it in such a way as to save all the souls that he had seen tethered to the dark soul in the center of Morag's laboratory. A fate that he had almost shared with them. He couldn't stand the thought of leaving any of them behind.

He saw the star spirit's light flicker. As she fell from the sky, he caught the star in his arms. Her spindly arms were over one of his strong demon arms and her legs over the other. Her non-corporeal form weighed nothing, but Trevi knew that she was still there. She looked up into his eyes and raised a weak hand to his cheek. "Thank you, Trevi, for becoming the 'Gardener of the Stars'. You've given the stars themselves hope."

Trevi felt a tingle from within followed by a sharp slice of severance. He gasped but did not drop the star in his arms as she darkened even more, and her shape began to flicker away. She moved no longer, her body limp and languid. Her eyes were closed, and her head tilted to the side. He could feel himself morphing back into his human form.

"What did you do, star spirit?" He asked the unconscious and fading form in his arms before halting his transition into a human and choosing to remain a demon. He needed to be able to see what little was left of her if he were to save her and the starflower. He felt barriers broken down inside of him that had always been there. He had an inkling that he could change back into a human any time that he desired, but experimentation with that would have to wait. He looked at the starflower behind him. The light was gone, and its petals were beginning to wilt. He knew what he had to do. The book had told him how. Trevi had saved Brook, and now, Trevi would save the star spirit and her beloved starflower.

CHAPTER 12: AMBUSH IN A BUSH

 aywren was quiet when Brook arrived with Auraline hidden in the brush at the edge of Elder's Clearing. You would never suspect that anything was amiss with the town if you didn't already know. If Morag hadn't been stealing the souls of others to feed his own life, while hiding his operations in a secret laboratory, and practicing a dark magic that he helped forbid others from dabbling in, one could have said that he had done a relatively good job at keeping Waywren peaceful and happy over the years. They were not at war with anyone and were happy keeping to themselves in the secluded comfort of the woods.

Their plan was a simple one. Auraline insisted that simple plans were more likely to succeed than extravagant ones. Auraline would go into Elder's Clearing alone and visit the village elder's hut to have a conversation with Renier, just like she had many times in the past before she had left Waywren for good. Most of the village should know who she was, and her presence would make a stir. They knew Emmy was back in town already, and that she was also staying in the village elder's hut. It was a good distraction for the town. Auraline's appearance would likely draw out Morag as well.

Brook was to remain hidden in the shadows and bushes until he had a good shot at Morag. Once he did, he would shoot a beam of starfire at him sniper-style, and that should be the end of it. Brook was to leave before anyone saw him. Auraline and Emmy would be left to clean up whatever mess remained in the wake of Morag's death to get Waywren back to a normal state where everyone could think for themselves and the village elder was in charge of keeping the peace. Their rendezvous waypoint would be Jax's cellar where Trevi would also be returning to once he completed his journey to the starflower.

"Good luck," Auraline whispered before she made her way toward the main path entrance to Elder's Clearing. It would look less suspicious if she didn't hop out of the woods. Brook nodded his thanks and waved goodbye to her. He watched her disappear from his view and began to get nervous. His palms were sweaty, and he felt uncharacteristically warm. Everything that could go wrong started to fill his mind and paralyze him. What if Morag wasn't in his hut like Auraline thought he was? What if Emmy was hurt? What if they attacked Auraline once she appeared? What if…

Brook shook himself. No. He couldn't let himself devolve into a worried mess now. Too much was riding on his success. The ring glowed on his finger. It was bright with starfire since he had stayed out later that night to absorb more starlight. As long as he could channel it toward Morag when he appeared, then everything would go perfectly.

An anciently hoarse voice cackled in mockery from behind Brook, "What if Morag is right behind you? Boy, you shouldn't mumble to yourself, someone might hear you." A sack was thrown over his head and his arms and legs were deftly bound together while Brook kicked and yelled in surprise. The ring was slipped from his finger by Morag's hand in the process of binding him, and Brook began to panic. "There's no need for that now, boy. You see, most of the town is out hunting your demon friend, Trevi. Not that they will find him since he is on his way into the Alveni mountains in search of the starflower, but I haven't a good way to recall them. They'll tire eventually and come home." Brook could feel himself being towed somewhere while they conversed.

"How do you know all that?" Brook asked genuinely surprised at what Morag knew of their plans.

"Oh, silly boy, do you really think I wouldn't know where Jax Pellon's house was? He was the first of your ancestors that I cursed. I killed him, you know. I still remember it after all these years. I used his blood to curse the rest of your family line." Morag's voice turned coy, "I let his boy 'sneak' back onto Krael after his mother passed away. It was one of my more fun and clever endeavors, you know. I figured that if I let your family bloodline live to be forty before I called upon their souls to return to me, then you would bear children who would also live to be forty, and then I would have a constant farm of life for my eternal life curse, augmented, of course, by my one-off findings on Alir."

Brook noted how proud of himself that Morag

seemed so he asked him a question in hopes to make this monster feel guilty, "How could you ruin so many people's lives just to make your life longer?"

Half-baked excuses started pouring out of Morag's mouth, "I am integral to the ecosystem of Alir. I keep peace with the green witches, and in turn, many others live in peace. My life is far more important than others."

Brook retorted, "How do you know that one of my family couldn't have played an important role in some other realm? There are other places at war, you know, it's not like your existence has brought peace to the universe. It's only in your little bubble that you see every day, and it's not true peace if the villagers can't even think freely. They are just your puppets. They are toys that you play with over the years."

Morag sneered his response, "Ah, the boy thinks he is a smart one, does he? Well then, I'll just have to admit the truth to you. I *wanted* to live forever, and all other excuses aside, this was the only way. I'm not sorry about it, either." Morag cackled with an evil glee that Brook could not comprehend.

Brook found himself dumped unceremoniously onto the ground. His backside hurt from the sudden collision. The sack was ripped off his head, pulling his hair in the process. He looked around the room that he was in to see what could only have been the secret laboratory that Trevi had described to him. It was more morbid than Brook could have imagined with the dead bodies preserved in clear liquids and the wretched aroma that filled his nostrils. Morag, in the dark folds of his cloak, moved over the table on the far side of the room and placed Brook's ring there. Brook would have to cross the length of the room to get it.

"Hey, smart boy. Now that you know all of this, do you know what I'll do to you, hm?" Morag continued to toy with Brook.

"Kill me?" Brook said abruptly.

"Oh, no. Very wrong. Why would I kill the soul farm that I've set up? No, I will have to erase your memory. But before I do, in my infinite kindness, I will show you the souls of your ancestors to put your mind at ease with how good they are being taken care of." With those words, Morag opened up a door near where Brook was sitting on the floor. Morag's ancient hand slipped out of his dark robes and pulled Brook to his feet to drag him inside the door. Brook knew that Morag wasn't showing him this out of kindness. He was doing it out of the joy that he was getting out of gloating to someone.

The smell made him throw up. Brook hoped that Morag would slip in it or would at least have the fun of cleaning it up later. Sadly, he had missed retching on Morag himself.

"What's wrong boy? Can't stand the smell of decaying bodies? Well, I guess it grows on someone after a few years." Morag disdainfully judged Brook.

"Look up, boy," Morag ordered in a tone that was accustomed to being obeyed. Brook did as he was told, out of curiosity as much as out of fear. He saw the glowing light of the white souls surrounding him along the walls that Trevi had described. The one on the end of the lowest shelf called to him. He looked in its direction as tears wet his eyes and a lump of tangled emotions choked his throat. Trevi had told him that his father was here and that he would know him, but a part of Brook hadn't really believed that it could be possible, until now. He had hoped, but he didn't believe. Now he believed. He felt the resolve fight its way to the top of his cocktail of emotions. He would save his father from his awful fate.

"So, you can sense your father's soul. How interesting," Morag noted Brook's reaction as though he were a science experiment.

"Can I touch him?" Brook asked with a slight quiver of emotion in his voice. More out of instinct than having any real idea what to do if he was able to touch his father again.

Morag looked down at Brook through his robes and didn't stop Brook from inching toward the ball of light. Brook figured that was as much of an agreement to move forward as he was going to get. Brook outstretched his hand, and Morag suddenly screamed, "No! What is happening?" He made a grab at Brook's hand to knock it down, but whatever was happening must have continued because Morag had forgotten about Brook and had gone to the larger, darker ball of light in the center of the room.

Brook realized that whatever was happening likely had to do with moon magic. He wouldn't be able to see it now because his ring wasn't on. Something clicked in Brook's mind: his ring. In Morag's distraction, Brook was able to stumble back into the previous room and snatch his ring off of the table. He eagerly put it back on and looked back into the room with the captured souls. There were severed misty, dark grey threads wiggling around from the dark, center soul. Those threads must have been connected to the creature's souls that surrounded the room. The bright lights on the shelves around the room started to turn into white, silvery wisps dissipating out of the room toward any exit that they could find. The souls were returning to their homes.

Brook raised his ring to point at Morag during his sudden panic and hasty ministrations to fix what had been broken. Brook willed the starfire to escape the ring and destroy the evil that was before him. He felt his hand jerk back slightly before a beam of bright, glowing starfire escaped the confines of the ring. Brook had to close his eyes to not be blinded by the light as he held his hand steadily aimed at Morag. Morag's screams intensified as the starfire engulfed him. There was nothing he could do to combat it. The starfire took effect too quickly. The dark, black soul in the middle of the room started to evanesce. When the ring had emptied itself of starfire, all that was left in the room was a dark cloak piled upon itself in the middle of the floor. Morag, shaman of Waywren village and commander of dark moon magic, had been defeated.

EPILOGUE

The Alveni mountains were not for the faint of heart, but no one could accuse Trevi of being cowardly. He had found a habitable precipice for his new garden where the bitter bite of the winds was muzzled by slabs of towering stone. It sat atop a large flat of rock that gazed directly into the sky, which Trevi understood to be ideal for starflowers based on what he had read in the gardening book gifted to him by the star spirit. Right now, at the very highest point of his plot, sat the brilliant blue star flower that he had successfully transplanted.

Trevi gazed proudly out at his accomplishment. The star spirit had been right. It had been one of the most difficult things that he had ever done to save both her and her starflower, but having completed the task successfully, he felt a satisfaction that ran deep into his soul. He knew that a miniature version of the star spirit that had visited him when he found the starflower initially was curled up in a deep sleep blanketed by one of the big, floppy petals. She was being nourished and gaining back strength enough to bloom with the starflower at night once more.

Trevi fed and watered the flower and its tiny

humanoid occupant daily. In between those times, he had started to cultivate the ground for more starflowers. He had carefully gathered the seeds from the brilliant blue one and was preparing them in the special fashion that the book suggested. He would never tell the details of the ground and seed preparation to anyone, as warned him by the star spirit. No one would be able to tell the small intricacies of his preparations just by looking at his garden, so he could at least entertain visitors every so often if they were able to make the dangerous journey up the mountains.

He leaned against the open doorway of the small wooden cabin that Emmy and Auraline had insisted that the green witches of Waywren help him to build. Outside of that, they had done an admirable job of settling the town back down. Thankfully, Morag had indeed only been mind-nudging the townsfolk and hadn't permanently altered anyone's mind. This made the transition of power back to Renier, the true village elder, quite simple with the removal of Morag.

Auraline and Emmy still spent much of their time in their own homes outside of Waywren, as they had become rather attached to them, but it was not uncommon to see them at Waywren for a visit. Renier and Auraline had gotten passed their differences. Even Lumeni, Auraline's light dragon familiar, had been able to dig out caverns connecting her usual home with the caverns that Morag had used for transportation of his secret items needed for his laboratory in Waywren. The same secret caverns that Morag had dragged Brook through on his way to his secret laboratory. They had seen to it that Morag's hut in Waywren was burned to the ground, destroying all evidence of the dark moon magic that he dabbled in along with it.

Brook and his father had moved off of Krael and onto Alir. It seemed fitting that they live in the home of their ancestors, so they rebuilt the house over the cellar where Jax's journal had been found. The secluded life that they had led on Krael while researching a cure to their curse had not garnered them many friends. There was not much for them to leave behind. Plus, Brook fancied Emmy, whether he liked to admit it or not. He wanted to be near her on Alir. Trevi had known Brook well enough to figure this sort of thing out without Brook having to confess anything to him. This is what happens when you've been brothers long enough. Shared blood or not.

Brook had stopped leaving traces of his memories around for people to find, but he didn't bother retrieving the one's that he had left scattered about either. He figured it would lead someone on a great adventure someday if they were to find his letters stowed away in the nooks and crannies of the wilderness. Brook still wrote though. He had always loved writing. Now he kept a journal that lived in his house as opposed to stuffing paper scraps into vials. He would scribe for Waywren on occasion as well.

And maybe, the most important thing to note about Brook was that he was finally opening himself to the notion that everything that was beautiful did not hide some sinister secret for him to find. He was starting to believe that some things were purely good in the world, and he wouldn't try to invent something about them to detract from their beauty and make them villainous in his eyes.

His father was just ecstatic to have his life back and would gratefully spend it helping Brook in whatever endeavors he had since he was the Pellon that finally broke the curse. Trevi chuckled to himself at that thought. Trevi himself was *technically* the one to break the Pellon's curse, but Spirit's flame the person that tried to rub that detail in Brook's face.

Siensa, the white dragon, would ferry Emmy and Brook up to see Trevi every so often. It was nice to see them when they came. Emmy loved that Trevi was becoming a gardener. She often gave him helpful tips on menial things and respected that he could not tell her many of the peculiar details of his garden.

In Trevi's opinion, Emmy's moon garden was far more splendid than his star garden. He had gotten to see the moon garden bloom in the moonlight while he had voluntarily occupied his demon form, and the show was utterly stupendous beyond words. He no longer feared the full moon; he revered it.

The ability to change back and forth between demon and human at will was exhilarating. He was so capable in his demon form, and he no longer had to suppress the constant aggression. He would almost have chosen to stay in that form continuously if he hadn't been so comfortable as a human. He could climb the mountains with ease, finding the magical necessities for his gardening with his heightened senses as he prowled around effortlessly. The demon was now his exalted superpower instead of his abhorrent curse.

When Trevi had spoken of the wonderment that he felt when gazing upon Emmy's moon garden to her and compared it to his beginnings of a star garden,

Emmy assured him that one day his star garden would outshine her moon garden. It was the nature of the stars to outshine the moon. The moon did not mind. The moon's glow had a magic of its own, so it did not need to be jealous of the stars. Trevi hoped that she was right. He would pour himself into this star garden until it was the grandest site on all of Alir. No star in the night sky would ever pass up the opportunity to shine in a starflower from Trevi's, the Gardener of the Stars', garden.

ABOUT THE AUTHOR

Aerospace Engineer by day, fantasy author by night, Theresa Biehle has never let increasing age or responsibility dampen the wilds of her imagination or prevent her from following her dreams. She grew up in the small town of Ida, Michigan playing backyard baseball, reading fantasy novels, taking juicy bites out of garden-fresh tomatoes after splashing through muddy creeks, and sneaking through cornfields to make wishes on magic trees before obtaining her Bachelor's Degree in Aerospace Engineering and a Master's Degree in Space Systems Engineering from the University of Michigan. Job availability herded her into Leesburg, Virginia where she resides now. Softball equipment now sits in her basement, fantasy novels cover her bookshelves, tomatoes grow in her garden, and she has never stopped believing in the power of wishes and dreams.

SOCIAL

Follow me here for information on future writing endeavors, or support me with a book rating/review!

Facebook: biehletheresa
Instagram: theresabiehle
Goodreads Author: Theresa Biehle
Website: **www.theresabiehle.com**

Newsletter signup and bookshop are available on my website.